The

MEMORY

Book

The

MEMORY

Book

A Novel

~

Penelope J. Stokes

W PUBLISHING GROUP™

www.wpublishinggroup.com

A Division of Thomas Nelson, Inc.
www.ThomasNelson.com

The Memory Book

© 2002 Penelope J. Stokes

Published by W Publishing Group, a division of Thomas Nelson, Inc., P.O. Box 141000, Nashville, Tennessee 37214.

This novel is a work of fiction. Names, characters, places, and incidents are either the products of the author's imagination or are used fictitiously. Any resemblance to actual events, locales, organizations, or persons, living or dead, is entirely coincidental and beyond the intent of the author or the publisher.

All poetry in *The Memory Book* is the original work of the author and may not be used without permission.

"Out of the Depths," hymn lyrics by Ruth Duck, ©1992 by GIA Publications, Inc. All rights reserved. Used by permission.

Library of Congress Cataloging-in-Publication Data

Stokes, Penelope J.
    The memory book : a novel / Penelope J. Stokes.
      p. cm.
    ISBN 0-8499-1706-9
    I. Title.

PS3569.T6219 M46 2002
813'.54—dc21
                                    2002066184

Printed in the United States of America

02 03 04 05 06 BVG 5 4 3 2 1

To Cousin Roena,
whom I never met,
but
whose Memory Book
fired my imagination
and inspired this novel

Prologue

October 1981

A cold autumn rain dripped from the ribs of a dozen umbrellas and splattered onto the red mud around the mourners' feet. Under a dull green canopy, a small girl sat swinging her legs against the metal folding chair and fiddling with a strand of curly brown hair. She watched intently as drops of mist gathered on her black patent leather shoes, merged, and dribbled off onto the lumpy rug of artificial grass under her feet.

For a moment the gray-haired woman seated next to her leaned forward as if to reprimand her for fidgeting, then put an arm around the girl and drew her close. Enduring but not returning the elder woman's embrace, the child allowed herself to be held for only a moment before going rigid. At last the old woman let go, and the girl settled into her seat, her dry eyes fixed upon the great bronze casket that stood like a sentinel, guarding the gaping hole that waited to swallow it up.

～

She didn't understand the words the minister was saying, but she tried to pay attention because her grandmother wanted her to. Something about lifting your eyes up to the hills, where help comes from. She raised her head, and in the distance, through the mist, she could see the soft rounded edges of purplish-blue mountains against a gray sky. She bit her lip and stared at the tops of the ridges, waiting for help to come.

But there was no help for her mother. She knew it, and nobody could tell her any different. She had been there, at the hospital. She had seen her mama go through the swinging doors with the big red cross on them. She had sneaked in and hidden behind a curtain, peeping out to watch as the people in white coats hovered over Mama and pounded on her chest and yelled orders to one another. She had heard the words *brain damage,* had seen the blood—lots of blood—slithering down the side of the table, puddling on the floor the way the rain puddled in low places. She had watched it slide out of her mother like water down a slow-moving drain, had heard the gasping rattle of her final breath.

Yesterday, at the funeral home, everyone had tried to be nice to her. They had stooped down to hug her and told her that her mama was safe and happy now, that her mama would feel no more pain, that Mama was in heaven with Jesus, that all things considered, it was a blessing Mama had died.

But Mama's death was not a blessing, and the Jesus she loved and trusted seemed very far away. While the doctors had worked, she had prayed—that the bleeding would stop, that Mama would open her eyes and get up off the table and take her to the park like other children's mamas. But Jesus hadn't heard her prayer; or if he had, he hadn't paid attention. The blood hadn't stopped. Mama hadn't gotten up.

She stared at the box, at the black hole, at the pile of dirt that was beginning to turn into a mountain of mud. That was where her mama was going—not to heaven, but into the ground.

She felt her grandmother take her hand, and she struggled to her feet and stood while people filed by, shaking hands and hugging both of them. She knew that everybody expected her to cry, but she couldn't make herself do it—not even for her grandmother's sake. She had used up all her tears there in the hospital, begging for Jesus to help. A whole ocean of them. And it hadn't done any good.

She turned away from the coffin and looked over her shoulder. On the far side of the cemetery, out in the pouring rain, a pickup truck had stopped. A man got out of the cab and stood with his shoulders hunched against the rain, watching. She tugged at her grandmother's sleeve, but before she could get her attention, the man ducked into his truck, shut the door, and drove away.

She looked back at the casket. It was over. Now all that was left was to put Mama in the ground, cover her up with the cold wet mud, and go home.

PART 1

Buried Memories

Only the shell
Can be dead and buried.
The soul lives on.
My hopes and dreams,
my fears,
my pain and longing
cling to me
like bittersweet perfume,
wafting their fragrance
on the breath
of eternity.

1

You Can't Go Home Again

P hoebe Lange leaned heavily on the rusting wrought iron gate and peered upward at the old Victorian house looming above her. How long had it been since she had been home—six months? Nine?

Too long. And not long enough.

A line from a graduate seminar on Thomas Wolfe flitted through her mind: "You can't go home again." Yet here she was.

The knot in Phoebe's stomach tightened. Her conscience reprimanded her for neglecting her grandmother, and she knew the voice inside her head spoke the truth. But even as she stood in front of the gate, she was aware that her avoidance of this house had nothing to do with lack of devotion. She loved these mountains, loved Asheville, loved Gram—and yet something inside her, something deep down and unreachable, resisted the inexorable pull of home. Too many memories. Too much confusion.

In Atlanta, two hundred miles and two decades removed

from the memories, Phoebe Lange was another person entirely—a person who had carved out a niche for herself. She hated the noise and the traffic and the seething anger that ran just beneath the skin of such a large city, but the anonymity suited her perfectly. Her life at the university was a product of her own creation. No longer was she the haunted, introverted child she had once been. She had re-created herself, become the vibrant, outgoing young woman she saw reflected in the eyes of those around her.

At Emory University, Phoebe had found everything she had ever wanted. Love, friends, a place of belonging. Intellectual challenge. A sense of purpose.

She had finally put the past behind her—so completely, in fact, that her fiancé, Jake Bartlett, teased her mercilessly about being a "mystery woman" who never talked about herself.

"I talk about myself all the time," she had protested the last time the subject had come up. "We talk about *everything*."

He shook his head. "We talk about life, literature, the law. Your studies and mine. We talk about books and movies and politics. Sometimes we even talk about theology. I know what you believe about all these things. I know your opinions—boy, do I know your opinions!" He chuckled and leaned forward intently. "I know what's in here—" He tapped a forefinger against his head. "But I often think I haven't even begun to fathom what's in here—" He moved his hand downward, indicating his heart.

Phoebe averted her eyes. "There's nothing much to know, Jake. I was an orphan, raised by my grandmother. I was so little when my mother died that I barely remember it. I'd just rather focus on the present and the future than dwell on the past."

"So you're not holding out on me, mystery woman? Hiding some terrible secret?" He grinned and rolled his eyes.

Phoebe laughed. "All right, you caught me. I'm busted." She let out a melodramatic sigh. "Before I came to college, I ran a brothel in my grandmother's house. Dealt crystal meth out of the trunk of my car. Laundered the money through Swiss bank accounts. I'm filthy rich, and on the run from the FBI."

"I thought it might be something like that." Jake shrugged. "I'm starving. Let's order pizza."

Remembering the conversation and the expression in Jake's eyes when he talked about wanting to know her heart, Phoebe took in a steadying breath. She hadn't counted on how vulnerable loving someone could make her feel. Emotions were so compelling, so raw and unpredictable. She was much more comfortable with intellect, with keeping things on a philosophical level. Yet Jake Bartlett had come into her life and invaded her heart before she'd had time to get her defenses up.

He was a passionate, persuasive man, open about his feelings, ever so sure of what he wanted out of life. And what he wanted, apparently, was Phoebe.

Being loved and wanted, Phoebe discovered, was a powerful enticement. She had fallen for him, hard. For the first time in her

5

life, she understood that image of "falling in love"—it was like missing the first step on a tall staircase, and being unable to stop your forward progress until you got to the end. Now the power of her love for him twined itself around the very roots of her soul, and the stronger it became, the more she found herself wanting to pull back, needing to reestablish a modicum of control.

Krista Carlson and Naomi Wilder, her closest friends, tried to reassure her.

Krista, a volatile redhead with a personality to match, launched into her usual cheer-me-up routine. "It's nothing more than premarriage jitters," she declared when Phoebe confessed her doubts. "Everybody gets them. Jake Bartlett is one in a million, and you know it. He's intelligent and sensitive—not to mention really, really cute, with that mop of blond hair and those fabulous blue eyes. Besides, he adores you. If I were in your shoes, I'd lasso him and drag him to the altar before he has a chance to change his mind." She laughed. "Come to think of it, if you decide you *shouldn't* marry him, I'd take him off your hands in a heartbeat."

Naomi, the serious, thoughtful one of the group, had a different perspective on the situation. "It may simply be cold feet," she agreed reluctantly, "but you owe it to yourself to find out. You've been concentrating on nothing but your thesis for months now, and you haven't really given yourself time to absorb all these changes in your life and consider what you want for the future. Perhaps it would do you good to take some time off, to be alone and discover what your heart wants to tell you."

Krista let out a little snort. She made no secret of the fact that she thought self-examination—or "navel gazing," as she called it—to be an utterly fruitless and time-wasting venture.

Phoebe, however, suspected there might be a good deal of wisdom in Naomi's suggestion. Time away, alone. A chance to evaluate what she was feeling. The opportunity to take a good hard look at what she wanted for her life, without the distraction of Jake's smoldering gaze on her. It was too hard to think with him around. Her feelings clouded her judgment and interfered with her reason.

So, in the end, she had accepted Naomi's advice, rejected Thomas Wolfe's, and come home to Asheville. To Gram. To the house that held the buried memories of her lonely childhood.

She gazed at the tall gables again, trying to steel herself to go inside. It had seemed like a good idea, taking time to sort things out, but now that Phoebe was here, she questioned the wisdom of that judgment. She felt herself shrinking, turning back into the angst-ridden, shadowed child who had grown up within these walls. No wonder she stayed away, back in Atlanta, where she could live the persona she had so painstakingly created.

Gram, to give the old woman credit, was not the kind of grandmother who insisted upon being pampered and coddled and taken care of. On the contrary, she firmly believed that young people had their own lives to live, their own decisions to make that ought not to be interfered with.

"Don't give a second thought to your old gram," she had said when Phoebe had phoned on Easter Sunday, apologizing profusely for not being there. "Finish your thesis. Study for your exams. I'll come down for graduation, and if you like, you can come back with me and we can spend some time together then."

May had arrived and with it graduation—a day marked more by relief than celebration. As it turned out, Gram had not been able to make the four-hour drive from Asheville to Atlanta to attend the ceremony. "It's only a cold," Gram had said, her voice sounding weak and breathless on the telephone, "but I'm afraid the trip is just too much for me. I'm so sorry, sweetie—I really wanted to come."

Her grandmother's absence from commencement had motivated Phoebe to follow Naomi's advice and get some time to herself. But it wasn't until ten days after graduation that Phoebe finally wrapped up loose ends in Atlanta and was ready to go home. When she called to tell Gram she'd be there on the sixth of June, Gram sounded so frail, so weak. Not at all like her old self.

"I'm worried," she confessed to Jake.

"Your grandmother is a tough old bird. She'll probably outlive us all," he said with a grin. "But it's a good time for you to go. The job search can wait. Take some time off. Go home to Asheville for a week or so. Don't worry about me. I'll be here when you get back."

Phoebe threw together a few things—some jeans and shirts, a couple sweatshirts, one or two nicer outfits. She had always packed light, and this time she didn't intend to stay very long. When she had finished, Jake followed her out to the car and put the suitcase in the trunk.

"Drive carefully," he said. He leaned down and kissed her, a kiss that nearly made her change her mind about going. "I'll miss you. Call and let me know how things are going."

"I will." With her heart turning to a lump of lead in her chest, she had pulled out of the driveway, watching in the rearview mirror as he got smaller and smaller. Then she turned the corner, and he finally disappeared altogether.

In all the memories that made up Phoebe's childhood, the house stood tall and bright and proud, like the pictures in the old photograph album, its wide, open porch welcoming, its many gables reaching to the sky.

But now it looked gray and weather-beaten, its paint peeling, one of its upstairs shutters tilting crazily. Had it looked this bad the last time Phoebe was home? Or had Phoebe simply seen what she'd wanted to see?

Taking a deep breath, Phoebe gripped her suitcase and made her way up the walk to the front door. High above, a curtain dropped back into place in a second-story window. Phoebe rang the bell, waited, then rang again.

She was just digging in her purse for her key when the front door swung open to reveal a scowling, hatchet-faced matron in a white uniform. "Yes?" the woman demanded. "What do you want?"

"I'm Phoebe Lange. Who are you?"

The woman didn't answer, but stood stock-still, blocking the doorway. "The granddaughter from Emory. Right. Well, I suppose you'd better come in."

Phoebe pushed past her into the entry hall. All the curtains were closed against the afternoon sun, and the house held a musty, closed-up smell. *The scent of death,* Phoebe thought briefly. Just as quickly, she pushed the idea aside and glanced around. Everything was familiar and yet different from the way she remembered it. The flowered wallpaper had begun to buckle. The oak floor was dusty, and the worn floral carpet looked as if it hadn't seen a vacuum in months. Every upholstered surface was covered with cat hair. In the corner, the curved-glass china cabinet, which had always been Phoebe's favorite, was cobwebbed to the wall as if some giant spider were saving it for a special dinner party. Phoebe sighed in dismay, then squared her shoulders doggedly.

"I'm the nurse," the woman said. "Name's Agnes Hargraves."

"I can see you're a nurse. What are you doing here?"

"Taking care of your grandmother, of course."

Phoebe frowned. "Since when does Gram need a keeper?"

"Since she came down with pneumonia."

All the air went out of Phoebe's lungs. "Pneumonia? She said it was a cold. When did this happen?"

Hargraves shrugged. "Three weeks ago. The antibiotics are helping, but she's very weak."

Phoebe stood there, rooted to the carpet while guilt sucked her under like quicksand. A cold, Gram had said. Phoebe should have known something was wrong, should have come sooner.

She opened her mouth to ask more questions, but the nurse had already turned her broad white backside and was lumbering unceremoniously toward the French doors on the opposite side of the parlor.

"This way," Hargraves muttered, as if Phoebe would not know the way to her own grandmother's bedroom. The nurse started up the oak stairway with Phoebe trailing behind. At the top, she stumbled over a huge gray tabby cat who slept on the landing. "Move, you beast!" Hargraves said, giving him a poke with her foot.

The cat, unharmed but startled, jumped up with a yowl and began to twine its body in a figure eight around Phoebe's ankles. "Scooter, you old sweetheart," Phoebe said, picking him up and rubbing him under his chin until he began to purr like a muffled motorcycle engine. "I've missed you! You doing all right, huh? How come you're not in bed with Gram?"

Hargraves turned and scowled in Phoebe's direction. "Animals are not allowed in the patient's room."

Phoebe's temper flared. "The *patient*," she said, "is my grand-mother. And Scooter is just as much a part of this family as I am."

"Humph," said Hargraves, and stomped ahead to Gram's room, leaving Phoebe and Scooter to follow or stay put. What they chose clearly didn't matter to her.

~

Down the dark hallway, at the end of a corridor of closed doors, one room stood open. Hargraves bustled about, tidying the tray of medicines. In the massive fourposter bed, propped on pillows and covered with a satin comforter, lay Gram. Her eyes were shut, her breathing heavy and labored. Phoebe said nothing for a moment, watching in silence as her grandmother's gnarled fingers gripped the comforter. Her skin looked brittle and transparent as old parchment.

How had it come to this? The last time Phoebe had seen her grandmother, she had been wearing jeans and sneakers and an old straw hat, and was headed out to tend the garden behind the garage. Even at seventy-nine, Gram had always looked and acted ten years younger. Every day she walked two or more miles along the treelined streets that surrounded the old house on Edwin Place.

Now, somehow, while Phoebe wasn't paying attention, her grandmother had turned into an old woman. And at the moment, a very sick old woman.

At last the watery blue eyes opened, and a tiny smile cracked the wrinkled face. "Phoebe, my dear!" the old voice whispered. "You've come at last."

"I'm here, Gram." Phoebe's voice cracked, and she reached out to take the withered hand in her own.

The touch seemed to give Gram strength, and she turned her head toward her granddaughter. Her eyes never left Phoebe's face. "Thank you, Hargraves."

"But, Mrs. Lange—" came the protest. The wrinkled hand waved her from the room. Shooting a venomous glare in Phoebe's direction, the nurse walked out and shut the door behind her.

Gram smiled weakly and sank back onto the pillows, still clutching Phoebe's hand. "She's a good soul," the old woman said quietly, "but a bit overbearing. You'll have to take her in hand."

"I will, Gram," Phoebe answered with more certainty than she felt. She had no doubt about the overbearing part. Where the good soul was buried, Phoebe couldn't begin to imagine.

"Would you open the curtains, my dear?" her grandmother said. "Hargraves keeps everything so dark and stuffy. She seems to think that shutting out the world will improve my condition. But you are here, and I must see you."

Phoebe went to the window and pulled back the heavy satin curtains. A yellow early-summer sun filtered in through the unwashed windowpane. "Now come over here," Gram commanded. Phoebe obeyed immediately and sat lightly on the side of the bed.

A thin, veined hand rose from the comforter and caught Phoebe under the chin, turning her face toward her grandmother. The grasp was firm, the grip tender but immovable.

"Look at me. Are you all right?"

A flinch in her gut caused Phoebe to avert her eyes. "Sure, Gram, I'm fine," she said. "I'm sorry you missed graduation. I would have come sooner if I'd known you were this ill."

"I know you would have, child. That's why I didn't tell you."

"What does the doctor say?"

Gram rolled her eyes. "Doctors *practice* medicine," she said. "I'm never quite convinced they have it perfected. If you must know, she says that at my age pneumonia can be dangerous. I've responded pretty well to the antibiotics, so she hasn't insisted on putting me in the hospital. I just hadn't counted on how long it would take to get well."

"But you *are* going to get well," Phoebe said, forcing herself not to turn the statement into a question.

"Am I going to die, you mean?" Gram laughed. "Yes, I'm going to die. Eventually. But I have no plans to do so in the immediate future."

A nervous laugh escaped Phoebe's lips. She exhaled heavily and began to relax a bit. Gram was sick, but she was still Gram. The realization brought a measure of comfort and security. Not enough, but a little.

"You look different," Gram was saying. "You're thinner. And your hair—"

"I haven't had a chance to get it cut." Phoebe ran a hand through the disheveled curls. "I've been"—she groped for a word—"preoccupied."

Gram struggled with the pillows for a moment, trying to sit up straighter. Even such a small effort seemed to exhaust her. She leaned back and closed her eyes.

"If you need to rest, I can come back later," Phoebe said.

"You'll do no such thing. We haven't seen each other in ages, and we need to talk."

The slough of guilt sucked Phoebe a little further down, and she looked away. "Gram, I feel so bad about not being here for you."

"What time is it?"

Phoebe frowned and glanced down at her watch. "It's two-fifteen. Why?"

"I was just wondering how long you intended to beat yourself up about having your own life."

Phoebe stared at her, then chuckled. "You're right, of course. I should be thinking about you and how you are feeling."

Gram shook her head. "No. I mean it. How long? Will ten minutes do? Fine. I'll wait ten minutes while you feel bad, and then maybe we can get on with our conversation." She closed her eyes.

Phoebe sat on the edge of the bed. Silence descended over the room, broken only by the soft tick-tick of the clock and the shallow wheezing sound of her grandmother's breathing. A memory pushed to the forefront of her mind—a faint recollection from her childhood. Even in Phoebe's earliest days in this house, Gram had had a habit of being candid and direct with her, an honesty usually tempered with a healthy dose of humor. Phoebe might second-guess herself, but she always knew exactly where she stood with Gram, and she didn't have to exert unnecessary energy playing mind games. Gram was the one person in her life that Phoebe trusted implicitly, and that trust had given her a small cocoon of security in a frightening and uncertain world.

After a while Gram opened one eye. "Is our time up?"

Phoebe looked at her wrist. "It's been eight and a half minutes, but I'll forgo the last minute and a half if you will."

Gram reached out and patted her hand. "Agreed. Now, tell me about graduation and about your plans."

"Graduation wasn't anything special. They held it outdoors on the Quad, and it was beastly hot. I nearly fell asleep a couple of times. The only exciting moment was when a crow started dive-bombing the president of the college up on the platform. That was pretty funny."

"But it *was* special. My only granddaughter received her master's degree."

Phoebe nodded. "Yes."

Gram peered at her. "You don't sound particularly thrilled. I thought this was what you'd always wanted—an M.A. in literature, the chance to teach, to open young minds to new and potentially life-changing ideas."

Phoebe took in a breath and held it for a second. "Sure, it's what I wanted. But things have gotten a little confusing. Jake has asked me to marry him."

Gram's lips turned up in the shadow of a smile. "He's a good man. You could do worse."

The understatement caught Phoebe by surprise. Gram adored Jake, and Phoebe knew it. "There's something you're not saying."

Gram raised one eyebrow. "Is there? Or is there something *you're* not saying?"

Phoebe shook her head. "I'm not sure I'm ready to get married. At least not right now." The answer was a hedge against the truth, but the truth was beyond Phoebe's ability to articulate. How could she possibly explain feelings she didn't understand herself?

Gram took a sip of water from a glass on the bedside table, leaned back against the headboard, and impaled Phoebe with a glance. "Be sure."

The simple sentence echoed in Phoebe's head with the force of a prophetic oracle. She didn't know how to respond, so she busied herself rearranging Gram's pillows. "You seem tired. Do you want me to leave?"

"Not quite yet. I'll need to rest in a bit, but first tell me about yourself. I want to hear more about what's been going on in your world."

Phoebe resumed her seat and cast about in her mind for something to say—something that would skirt around the uncertainties that had been gnawing at her for weeks. "Well, let's see—Jake has just passed the bar and taken a position as an associate at Baker, Mason, & Woods. Family law, a Decatur firm near Emory. Very promising."

Gram waved a hand to indicate that she should continue.

Phoebe rambled on for a while, flitting from one subject to the next. She talked about Jake, about her comprehensive exams, about the weekend trip she and Krista and Naomi took down to Milledgeville to visit Flannery O'Connor's grave, about her thesis on metaphysical imagery in the poetry of George Herbert. About anything except herself. All surface, all superficial. Small talk at a cocktail party.

At last, she ran out of words. She glanced up and saw that her grandmother looked paler and more drawn than she had earlier.

"You're exhausted, Gram."

"I am a little tired. Maybe I do need to rest for just a while." She began to cough, a deep, rattling sound.

Hargraves appeared in the doorway. "It's time for your medicine, Mrs. Lange."

"All right." Gram turned her eyes toward Phoebe. "We'll resume this conversation later, dear. You are staying, aren't you?"

"Of course. As long as you need me." Phoebe kissed her grandmother on the cheek and escaped into the hall. Hargraves closed the door firmly behind her.

2

Things That Go
Bump in the Night

Phoebe leaned against the wall and exhaled a pent-up breath. Outside the sanctuary of Gram's room, she had the sense of being an interloper on unfriendly terrain. At any moment she expected the Battle-axe to reappear and evict her from the premises.

And yet this was her home. After Mama's death, Phoebe had come to live with her grandmother. She had grown up here, told her secrets and dreams and ambitions to these walls. She belonged here. Why, then, did she feel like an alien in her own skin?

Straightening her shoulders, she forced herself down the dark hall. As she went, she opened the doors on either side of the corridor and looked into each of the rooms. Adjacent to her grandmother's room was the library, furnished with a scarred mission oak table and a collection of comfortable leather chairs. The walls were lined floor to ceiling with books of all kinds.

Across the hall and around a corner from her grandmother's

room, Phoebe entered what had been her bedroom before she had gone off to college—a large, spacious chamber with windows on three sides. The northeast tower. The window to the left faced west, overlooking an enclosed courtyard. The other two windows faced north and east, overlooking the corner of Edwin and Magnolia. As a child, Phoebe had been afraid of this room, claiming that the moonlight coming in from all sides made creepy shadows at night. But later, as a teenager, she had taken it for her own. Coming back to it comforted her now.

When the few wrinkled clothes she had brought were safely stashed, nearly lost in the expanse of the huge oak wardrobe, Phoebe lay down across the bed. She hadn't realized how tired she was. Her back ached with pent-up tension. She pulled a corner of the coverlet over her feet and tried to rest.

But Gram's weary and withered face loomed before her each time she closed her eyes, and the enormity of her personal quest to find herself overwhelmed her. *God,* she thought miserably, *what am I doing here?*

It was not a prayer.

Phoebe couldn't remember the last time she had truly prayed.

She had always believed in God—or tried to. Even as a child, facing the horrible fact of her mother's death, she had managed to hold onto faith in a God who loved her and cared for her.

Mama had been thirty-two years old when her lifeblood had drained away on the floor of a hospital emergency room. Phoebe could still remember the sight of that blood, could still hear the whining squeal of the heart monitor, screaming that her mother's pulse had stopped forever.

The doctors who had tried to save her shook their heads and said it was a blessing that she had died. The same sentiment had been offered again at the visitation, and a third time at the funeral. Maybe Phoebe was supposed to believe it simply by virtue of repetition, but if redundancy was intended as inoculation against the pain, the overdose didn't take. Even at age five, Phoebe knew better.

It was Gram who told her that God was not to blame for her mother's death, that terrible things happened in this world. All those well-meaning people who said that Mama's death was a blessing were simply giving an easy answer to a very difficult question.

Phoebe spent the early years of her formation riding on her grandmother's spiritual coattails. Gram knew what it meant to be honest with God. She never minced words with the Almighty. She believed that God was big enough to shoulder her questions, her anger, her pain.

It was an important lesson, but one that became increasingly difficult for Phoebe to master, especially second hand. As she grew out of childhood, left the sanctuary and shelter of her handed-down faith, and began to grope her way toward her own spiritual truths, Phoebe discovered that preachers and Sunday school teachers and other religious professionals seemed determined to stifle her insistent questions. They offered pat answers instead of thoughtful dialogue.

Phoebe quickly got the message: Good Christians kept their doubts to themselves. They buried their pain so as not to embarrass God. They made excuses for unanswered prayer. Good Christians didn't ask questions about whether God was dependable, or why suffering had to happen if God supposedly loved them.

Faith meant you didn't rock the boat. Asking *why* meant you didn't trust God.

And so Phoebe kept quiet. In public, anyway. She went through the motions, attending church and keeping up the appearance of religion, but she rarely found a spirit like her grandmother's among the good Christians who sat next to her in the pews.

Until she met Jake Bartlett.

His experience with a dominating minister-father had so jaded him that for a while he had abandoned the church altogether. When he came back to the fold, his faith was stronger and more authentic than any Phoebe had ever seen. He understood questions and doubts and anger with God, and he had no qualms about expressing those feelings. For Jake, faith and doubt were not enemies, but allies. He trusted God fully, even in the midst of unanswerable questions.

Although at times it made her profoundly uncomfortable, Phoebe respected his faith. She envied it.

But she couldn't imitate it. Her questions were too difficult, her pain too deep even for God.

Phoebe Lange was no atheist. She still believed.

She just had so little to say to God these days.

⁓

Someone was knocking on Phoebe's door. She struggled into wakefulness, every gesture painfully slow. Her right arm, pinned under her on the bed, was asleep. She moved it carefully, wincing at the needle-points of pain that stabbed into her palm as she flexed her fingers.

The light in the room had shifted and dimmed. What time was it? How long had she slept? Phoebe ran one hand over her cheek to push back her hair; her face was pocked with the design of the chenille bedspread.

The persistent knocking continued. Shaking her head to clear her mind, she rolled off the bed and stumbled toward the door.

Hargraves's scowl greeted her as she opened the door. "Dinner's getting cold," the woman snapped. "Downstairs, in the kitchen."

Phoebe thrust her stocking feet into her shoes and followed the nurse down the hall to the back stairway. Here the steps were narrow and dark, curving into the kitchen entry. Still half-asleep, she stumbled and almost fell. Hargraves paid no attention, but clumped stolidly downward and disappeared around a corner. Phoebe, a few steps behind, entered in time to see Hargraves slinging dishes onto the square pine table against the outer wall of the room.

"Your grandmother's had her dinner an hour ago," Hargraves

muttered, cutting off the question that had begun to form on Phoebe's lips. "Sit."

Phoebe obeyed. The table contained several small bowls of leftover vegetables, a plate of plain white bread, and a large chunk of roast beef.

When Hargraves plopped her ample form into a chair and scraped it up to the table, Phoebe smiled wanly and reached for a slice of bread. But Hargraves stopped her midreach with a look as effective as a fork in the back of the hand. Folding her red knuckles together and bowing her head, the nurse murmured a table prayer, reciting the words so rapidly that Phoebe had no idea what they were. Only the punctuated "Amen" alerted Phoebe to the fact that the ritual had ended and the meal had officially begun.

Without prelude, Hargraves picked up the meat knife and began to slice the roast beef. Then suddenly, in the middle of a slice, she lifted the knife and pointed it at Phoebe. "I can't for the life of me understand young people," she said, her eyes fixing Phoebe's in a threatening gaze. "Why are you here?"

"What kind of question is that?" Phoebe burst out, exhaustion and tension finally getting the best of her. "I'm here because I love my grandmother."

Hargraves resumed slicing, but her eyes never left Phoebe's face. "Really."

"Yes, really."

Hargraves kept silent but continued staring until Phoebe

stammered, "And I've got some things to work out. Personal things. I needed some time to myself."

"At least that's a little more honest." She flung the knife down triumphantly and slapped a thick piece of roast beef onto Phoebe's plate.

The hair on the back of Phoebe's neck prickled. "I didn't know she was so ill."

"Ill or not, she needs her family."

Phoebe stifled the familiar rush of guilt. "I know. But I talked to Gram right before exams. She said she couldn't make it to graduation because she hadn't been able to shake a cold."

Nurse Hargraves lifted one eyebrow. "Humph."

"It's true. I do love her, and I would do anything for her."

"Anything?"

Phoebe nodded. "Anything." She leaned forward. "What can I do, Mrs. Hargraves, to help my grandmother?"

A strange look flashed across the older woman's face, as if she were seeing the ghost of a long-dead memory. Then the mask settled over her countenance once more. "Listen," she said. "Listen and trust."

～

Phoebe jerked upright in the bed, her mind swirling with images from a dream. Her mother's face. A hooded figure, standing in the rain. A shadow against the window. Bumping noises and a muffled cry.

She ran her hands through her hair and let out a deep breath. From somewhere deep in her memory, a childhood chant surfaced: *From ghoulies and ghosties and long-legged beasties, and things that go bump in the night, Good Lord, deliver us.*

Gram had taught her that prayer, almost twenty years ago, when Phoebe had first come to live here after Mama's death. Everything frightened her in those days—the creaking sounds of the enormous old house, the wind in the eaves, the thudding of acorns dropping on the roof overhead. And the dreams—especially the dreams.

Together they would recite the prayer, over and over again, until the funny sounds of words like *ghoulies* and *ghosties* and *beasties* sent them both into a fit of the giggles. Then Gram would stroke her hair and sing quietly to her until she fell asleep.

The memory of that protective touch soothed Phoebe's troubled heart, and she lay back down with her eyes wide open, watching the play of moonlight and shadow on the ceiling. A cool night breeze blew through the open window, and in the distance, she heard the bark of a dog and the faint ringing of a telephone.

Phoebe bolted up again. The phone! She had promised to call Jake as soon as she arrived. She grabbed the clock on the bedside table and stared at its luminescent dial. Two forty-five. Should she call him now or wait until morning?

She got up and rummaged in her bag for her cell phone, only

to find that the battery was dead. In this entire huge house, Gram only had two telephones—one downstairs in the hallway, and the other in her bedroom, an extension Phoebe had insisted upon when she went off to college. She drew on her robe and slipped down the stairs.

Jake answered on the second ring. "I'm glad you called," he said as soon as she had identified herself. "I've been worried about you."

"I'm sorry I didn't call sooner. I . . . I forgot."

There was a long pause. "You've been forgetting things a lot lately," he said. "And you've seemed . . . I don't know, kind of distant. As if something's going on with you that you can't talk about." His voice took on a husky, intimate tone. "I know you, Phoebe. I know when something's wrong."

A silent protest rose up in Phoebe's mind. How could he possibly know her when she didn't even know herself? He knew the image, the persona she'd created. And that was what he loved. The mystery woman. If she let him get closer, behind the mystery—

She pushed the thought away. "I'm fine."

A long silence stretched between them. At last he said, "All right." She could hear him sigh through the telephone. "How's your grandmother?"

"She has pneumonia. She's had it for three weeks."

"I'm sorry to hear that." His voice was gentle, compassionate. "Tell her we'll be praying for her, all right?"

"I will."

"And for you, too." She could almost see him leaning in to the receiver, his sky-blue eyes intense, his whole self focused on her. "Are you sure there's nothing you want to tell me?"

Phoebe hesitated. Then she said, "No, Jake. I'm OK, really I am. I just need to sort a few things out, do some journaling. Maybe this time away at Gram's will give me the opportunity to do that."

"All right. I'll call you tomorrow. I love you. I'll love you forever."

Forever? she thought. *Not likely.* She shut her eyes and swallowed down the lump in her throat. "I love you, too. Good night."

Phoebe hung up the phone and crept back up the stairs. Her head ached, and every nerve in her body felt taut and strained. She closed the door, turned on the light, and sat down on the bed. Yes, Jake loved her. So did Krista and Naomi. But they didn't know who she really was. They didn't know about the nightmares, the fear Phoebe herself could not explain. They had no idea of the need and weakness that lurked below the surface. With so many years of practice, she had learned to cover it well.

She reached into the drawer of the bedside table and pulled out the small vinyl-covered notebook that served as her journal. On the inside front flap, she had pasted a copy of one of George Herbert's poems. She read again the words she knew by heart, the offering of a seventeenth-century country priest:

A broken ALTAR, Lord, thy servant reares,
Made of a heart, and cemented with teares:

• • •

A HEART alone
Is such a stone
As nothing but
Thy pow'r doth cut.

Too well she knew the truth of Herbert's words—the stoniness of the human heart, the tears that cemented those stones in place. But experience had taught her something the poet apparently hadn't realized—that some hearts were too hard to be cut even by the power of God's love. Some wounds were past healing, some broken places beyond redemption. Some stones could never be made into altars.

Phoebe's eyes drifted to the title page of the journal, completely blank except for her name at the top and a brief line she had typed and pasted at the center. Another quotation, this one from a Jewish rabbi—a bit of wisdom she had gleaned years before from a long-forgotten source: "How can you claim to love me if you do not know what makes me weep?"

Exhaustion overtook her, and her hands began to shake. She shoved the journal back into the drawer and snapped off the light.

"From things that go bump in the night," she whispered as she collapsed into bed and pulled up the covers, "Good Lord, deliver us."

3

Family Secrets

Phoebe tossed restlessly for the remainder of the night and woke up at seven the next morning, exhausted but unable to will herself back to sleep. She went into the bathroom, brushed her teeth, then washed her face three times before she realized that the dark circles under her eyes were not the result of smudged mascara. "Bags," she muttered. "I'm too young for bags, and these are suitcases. Steamer trunks."

A shower made her feel a little more human, until she discovered that in her haste to leave Atlanta, she had neglected to pack a hair dryer. All that long curly hair lay heavy and damp on her shoulders, weighing her down. Had it been short and layered, the way she preferred it, she could have just brushed it back and let it dry naturally. But Jake liked it long.

Or did he? At the moment she couldn't quite remember if he had said so, or if she had simply projected that opinion upon him and attempted to please him without actually knowing his preferences. Either way, the capitulation added half an hour to her morning routine and no end of bother when she found herself without the right styling equipment.

With a grunt of disgust, she threw the hairbrush onto the vanity. It was hard work, not knowing for sure if she was loved for herself instead of for the image she projected. Exhausting, keeping up such facades.

Phoebe rooted through the drawers in the vanity. No blow-dryer. She did, however, come across a pair of scissors. Nice sharp scissors. She picked them up and held them to the light, snapping them open and shut. She had cut her hair herself all through undergraduate school, and done a pretty good job of it, too. Just a little trim here, a snip there, maybe.

Twenty minutes later, the heavy curls that had weighed her down littered the tile floor around her feet. She scooped them into the trash can, toweled the clippings off her shoulders, and shook her head. It was a good cut for an amateur. And she felt more herself than she had in months.

Phoebe replaced the scissors in the drawer, ran her fingers through her hair to fluff up the layers, and was just pulling on jeans and a polo shirt when she heard noises downstairs. Heavy footsteps crossing from the kitchen to the hallway. Then Hargraves's gruff voice yelling up the stairs.

"Phoebe! Breakfast!"

Phoebe dashed down in her bare feet and slid into a chair at the kitchen table.

Hargraves waited until Phoebe settled herself, then growled through the ritual of saying grace. She used the identical words in the same tone of voice as she had the night before, as if daring God to do anything less than bless this food that was set before them.

But maybe the prayer worked. At any rate, breakfast was considerably more appetizing than the supper leftovers she had eaten the night before. Hargraves had made bacon and scrambled eggs. Phoebe hadn't realized how hungry she was until the platter was nearly empty and she was spreading strawberry jam on her third piece of toast.

She looked up to find Hargraves staring at her.

"Is something wrong?" Phoebe asked.

"Nice haircut."

Phoebe smiled. Maybe the old Battle-axe was softening a bit. "Thanks, I, ah—" Then she stopped. Hargraves's expression had not changed a bit from that carved-in-stone countenance. She was surveying Phoebe with a cold eye, clearly not interested in chitchat.

"When you're finished, your grandmother would like to see you."

Phoebe's appetite vanished as fear edged in. Had Gram taken a turn for the worse?

Despite Hargraves's disapproving frown, Phoebe tossed her plate to the floor so that Scooter could lap up the remains of her eggs. Then she threw the half-eaten toast into the trash can and headed for the stairs.

When she reached the bedroom, panting slightly from the run up the steps and down the hall, her grandmother was sitting up in bed with pillows stacked behind her. She looked better this morning, stronger, not quite so frail, with a bit more color in her cheeks.

Apparently Gram could read the concern on her face. "This is not a deathbed summons," she said with a wry grin. "You can take the time to put on your shoes."

Phoebe looked down at her bare feet. "I'm OK."

"All right, then. Come sit." Gram patted the comforter and waited while Phoebe settled herself on the edge of the bed.

"Am I crowding you?"

"No, my dear, you're just fine." She took a sip of water from a glass on the bedside table, and Phoebe noticed that her hand trembled when she set it back. She studied her grandmother's face—the soft skin, webbed with wrinkles, the gentle brown eyes. She looked so frail. Tears clogged Phoebe's throat, and she couldn't speak.

"You're worried about me."

Phoebe nodded.

"This is a temporary setback, my dear, not a life-and-death battle. I'm feeling better every day. I'll be back out in my garden before you know it." She turned her head and gazed out the window for a moment. "But I have to admit, this little incident has made me more conscious of the brevity of life."

A knot of anxiety formed just below Phoebe's breastbone. "What do you mean?"

"Despite all my good intentions, I won't live forever," Gram said. "And given that difficult truth, there are some things I need to talk to you about before it's too late."

The knot swelled to the size of a grapefruit, and the bacon and eggs Phoebe had eaten for breakfast churned in the pit of her stomach. "All right," she managed. "What do you want to talk about?"

A strange expression came over her grandmother's face—a look Phoebe had never seen before. It might have been apprehension, but it almost looked like shame.

Gram mumbled something Phoebe didn't catch.

"Excuse me?"

Gram cleared her throat. "I said, it's about your father."

Phoebe's mind screeched to a halt. "My what?"

"Your father. My son, Jude." Gram lowered her eyes and picked at a loose thread on the comforter. "How much do you remember about him?"

Phoebe shrugged. "Not much, really. I vaguely recall him being there, off and on, when I was really little—maybe three or four. Then he was—well, just gone. Mama would never say much about him. And neither did you."

"And you didn't ask," Gram said quietly. "Why was that, Phoebe?"

"I suppose I . . . well, he was never really part of my life, was he? He died when I was so young. I remember once someone— at church, I think—saying it was a blessing he was gone. But since Mama never seemed to want to talk about him, I guess I just put him out of my mind, didn't think about him much."

Phoebe's answer was only half true. She had *tried* to put him out of her mind, but hadn't wholly succeeded. She thought of him less often as time went by, but he had always been there, in the back of her mind, hovering, haunting her. A vague image from early childhood. A memory better suppressed than explored. A dark faceless shape with intense, piercing eyes. Something about that shadowy memory frightened her, and so she pushed it down, deeper and deeper, until through long years of practice she succeeded in putting him out of her mind altogether.

Then a thought struck Phoebe, and she panicked. "What's this about, Gram? Are you sicker than you're letting on?"

Gram's face went white. She closed her eyes briefly and shook her head. Then, with a trembling hand she reached into the drawer of the bedside table and pulled out a rumpled newspaper clipping. "I hoped to spare you this," she murmured.

Apprehensively, Phoebe reached out and took the clipping from her grandmother's shaking hand. She spread it out on the bed and squinted at it. It was from the Asheville *Citizen-Times,* dated June 3, 2001. Four days ago.

JUDE LANGE TO BE RELEASED, the headline read.

Convicted murderer Jude Oliver Lange is scheduled to be released from custody after serving 20 years of a 25-to-life sentence. Lange's case made headlines in 1981, when he was convicted of attacking his estranged wife, Marie Lange, and beating her to death with a tire iron. The sheer brutality of the murder shocked the citizens of Asheville and all of Western North Carolina, and raised questions about the applicability of the death penalty in Lange's case. Protests against his release have already begun to flood into the governor's office.

Authorities revealed today that Lange's parole, denied repeatedly over the years, was finally granted on May 28. "This crime offends all civilized sensibilities," one officer reported. "He should be locked up for life." Other officials, however, claim that Lange has been "a model prisoner" and seems to pose no further threat to society. Lange's release has been set for later in June.

Below the article, two photographs appeared side by side: on the left, a grainy shot of Phoebe's mother, young and smiling, her blonde hair swirling around her shoulders—the very same picture

Phoebe kept in a frame on her dresser. On the right, a photograph of a man Phoebe had never known, yet nevertheless recognized. A man prematurely aging, his eyes recessed into deep sockets. Eyes like hers. Hair dark like hers.

Her father.

Her mother's killer.

⌒

Phoebe put the clipping down and stared, unseeing, at the face she had known and loved all her life. Gram. Her own grandmother. The woman who had always prided herself on absolute veracity. She had never skirted difficult issues, had always answered Phoebe's questions honestly, even when honesty hurt. If there was one thing in life Phoebe had always known she could depend upon, it was her grandmother's commitment to the truth.

"How could you possibly have kept this from me?" Phoebe fought to keep her indignation in check. "Did you think I wouldn't find out?"

"You believed he was dead. I thought it might be better—"

"But he *wasn't* dead. He was in prison—*for killing my mother!* And he's being released this month." Phoebe paused and summoned all her inner reserves. "Why didn't you tell me? For God's sake, Gram, he was my father! Your son!"

"Yes, he was my son," she said. "And I was ashamed of him. I was afraid for you." Her voice lowered, almost to a whisper. "He was a violent man."

The way Gram said those words, quiet, almost menacing, triggered something in Phoebe's brain. Her mind flooded with images from the past—nightmarish images, of her mother stretched out on a table in the ER, of blood pouring from the gaping wound in her skull, trickling into puddles on the floor. The blood metamorphosing into rivulets of mud, red mud dripping down the mound of earth next to the coffin. Someone whispering, "It's a blessing that she died." And one more long-buried memory—a brief glimpse of a man, standing over her mother, holding something in his hand. His head turning, his icy eyes staring at her.

"Then my mother's death was not an accident." The words came out of Phoebe as if they were spoken by someone else, someone composed and in control.

"No, it was not."

An eerie calm settled over Phoebe's heart, a numbness brought on by intense cold. She felt nothing. Not shock or outrage or debilitating agony. Only a detached curiosity, the interest of a literary analyst taking notes on the structure of a particularly compelling murder mystery.

"Perhaps I should know the details," Phoebe said. When her grandmother didn't respond, she prodded further, "My father left us when I was very small?"

"No. Your mother left him. You were three."

"Why?"

"She was afraid of him. He had—" Gram hesitated. "He had slapped her, shoved her around a time or two, when he had been drinking excessively. Once she had even called the police. Then one night he lashed out at you. She left and brought you here to stay with me for a while."

"That was exactly the right thing to do. You always tell an abused spouse to get herself and her children out of danger, and then the situation can be evaluated after a cooling-off period."

Gram nodded, her lined face set in a grim expression.

"Then what happened?"

"She had him arrested, and he was sentenced to ninety days in jail. The three months passed, and he was released, but he didn't come home. Eighteen months later, he returned with a story about getting his life together and wanting to reconcile with his family. I have to admit he seemed like a changed man. He said he had quit drinking, had a steady job, had rented a nice apartment. Your mother wanted to believe him. *I* wanted to believe him. He was so handsome, so charming, so . . . persuasive."

"She went back to him."

"Yes." Gram sighed. "And we know the rest."

"Mama didn't fall and hit her head. You always told me she hit her head." The words came out strained, wooden, and Phoebe closed her eyes against the image that continued to press up against her mind—those icy eyes in that dark shadowed face.

"It was a brutal attack," Gram said. "He tore up the apartment, tried to make it look like a robbery, but because of his previous record, the police weren't fooled. They caught up with him the night after the funeral, at a bar on the west side of town.

He tried to make a run for it, but he was drunk and crashed into a telephone pole. They brought him in and charged him with the murder. He confessed, said it was all his fault." Her thin frame shook visibly as a shudder ran through her. "They found the murder weapon—the tire iron from his pickup truck, covered with hair and blood—in the Dumpster outside the apartment building. The trial didn't take very long. He was found guilty, sentenced to prison—twenty-five years to life."

"And you didn't tell me because—"

"Because I wanted you to have a normal childhood. Or as normal as possible, considering the circumstances. I didn't want you living with that burden—being the little girl whose father killed her mother."

The horror of that final sentence barely penetrated. Phoebe's mind was still analyzing. "How did it happen, Gram? As I understand patterns of domestic violence, a man usually doesn't grow up to be an abuser unless he has seen it modeled, unless his own father—" She stopped suddenly and peered into her grandmother's eyes. "You?"

Gram began to weep silently. Tears ran down her cheeks, following the tracks of wrinkles. She wiped them away with the heel of her hand. "My husband, Lewis, your grandfather, was . . . well, not a demonstrative man. He had suffered a great deal in his young life. He lost his mother very young, and then his older sister, who was raising him, also died. When we married, I knew he had some hidden pain and anger. I just didn't know how much."

Phoebe forced her mind to stop taking notes for a moment. "You don't seem the type to be a victim of domestic violence. You're so strong and independent."

"I've changed a lot in the years since Lewis died. I was young when I married him—a child, really. In those days a woman's role was to be submissive, to expect her husband to take control. He never struck me, but he did threaten it. He was a very unhappy man. He yelled a lot, and I simply took it, tried to do better, tried to find ways not to make him angry." She exhaled heavily. "It was a relief when he died. But by then the pattern was established in Jude. He was grown. A man. A man just like his father."

"And with Jude—my father—the pattern escalated?"

"Yes. Helped along by regular doses of liquor."

Phoebe shut her eyes. It was too much to take in, this revelation about her family. Secrets hidden for years, decades of deception. Then a thought struck her—a terrible, incomprehensible idea.

"He wants to see me, doesn't he?"

"I don't know." Her grandmother lay back against the pillows and closed her eyes. "I haven't spoken to him in more than twenty years. I received a letter from the Department of Corrections informing me of his release, although it told me little more than what's written in the newspaper. But he may request to see you, yes."

"Never," Phoebe muttered through clenched teeth. "Never in a million years."

She left Gram's side, went out into the hallway, and slammed a fist against the wall. Bile churned up from her stomach into her throat, and for a minute Phoebe thought she was going to be sick. Then the tears began to flow—hot tears of rage and regret, tears linked to memories she had suppressed for the past twenty years. If that monster actually thought she would see him, that they would have a happy, long-awaited father-daughter reunion, he was out of his mind.

Some things were beyond forgiveness.

Some things just needed to stay buried.

4

The Sins of the Fathers

O nce Phoebe had left her grandmother's presence, her analytical facade began to lose its grip and the truth pressed in upon her with astonishing speed and force.

Mama's death had been no accident. Phoebe's father had murdered her—had beaten her brains out with a tire iron. He had cracked open her skull and left her bleeding to death on the living-room floor. The brutality of the images sickened Phoebe, made her want to retch. Yet she continued to call them up, one at a time, forced herself to look reality in the eye and call it by the ugliest name she could think of. Maybe if she faced this head-on, the horror of it would pass by quickly and give way to a matter-of-fact resignation.

But it didn't. The atrocity hovered over her, a full eclipse across the sun, midday turned to darkness by the crucifixion of something inside her.

The irony of her situation did not escape her. She had

returned here—to the place of her upbringing, to the grandmother who loved her—so that she could give herself time to explore who she was and what she wanted out of life. She had come home to find out about herself.

And what had she discovered? That the anxious, fearful child she had tried so hard to leave behind still existed, and had good reason to be anxious and fearful. That the stuff of her nightmares wasn't created out of a fertile imagination, but from a terrifying, traumatic reality.

In the past few months, Phoebe had struggled with some insecurities, particularly around her relationship with Jake. But the challenge of dealing with a few hesitations about marriage and some personal self-doubts paled in comparison with the issue that now loomed like an iceberg in her soul, threatening to sink her forever.

Who am I? Phoebe tried to consider the question logically, to convince herself that she was the same person now that she had been, before she had discovered that the blood of a murderer pumped in her veins. Nothing had changed, nothing except her perceptions. And yet she couldn't shake the sense that she was an alien being, that someone else occupied her skin. As if she had found out for the first time that her parents weren't really her parents, that she had been conceived by someone else entirely. As if, like an amnesiac, she had no identity—or none that she could get a grip on.

Phoebe knew what it meant to think of herself as an orphan,

to be the child whose parents had both died. But she had no idea how to live with this knowledge: *I am the child of a murderer*. In one terrible instant, the foundation of her self-image was irreparably shaken, and she no longer knew what truths would support her.

And another question plagued her as well, a question that pertained not so much to the past as to the present, and the future: *Who could she trust?* Phoebe had always believed that her grandmother, above all others, was a person who spoke and lived by truth. But Gram had deceived her—if not lied outright, at least committed a sin of omission, and a rather significant one. If she couldn't trust her . . .

Phoebe's thoughts trailed away, unable to bear the weight of the conclusion her mind proposed.

In a fog, she wandered into the library and sank into one of the overstuffed leather chairs near the window. She had to sort this out. An early rain had set in, and her mind began to move in rhythm with the sounds of water coursing down the glass panes and splashing against the sill.

During a social work internship in their junior year, Diana, Phoebe's college roommate, had enlisted her help with dozens of cases that chilled her soul. Situations involving all sorts of family dysfunction—alcoholism, drug addiction, child endangerment, molestation.

In one horrific case, a mother had kept her daughter chained up and locked in total darkness in an attic closet. Diana's job had been to protect the child. But in order to do that job effectively, she also had to understand the perpetrator. Upon further investigation she discovered that the mother herself had been savagely molested as a very young girl. To the woman's twisted, traumatized mind, locking her daughter in darkness was her way of protecting her child from a similar fate.

The mother's mental illness did not excuse such behavior, of course. There were never any excuses. But there were reasons, patterns that often went back for decades. And unless the pattern was broken by intervention and therapy and healing, it usually continued, a virulent disease eating its way through one generation after another.

A fragment of a long-forgotten Bible verse worked its way into Phoebe's mind: *The sins of the fathers are visited upon the children to the third and fourth generations . . .* It was not a threat of punishment coming from an angry, vengeful God. It was a statement of reality, a declaration of the way things were.

But why? Was a family's history fluid, like a river, so that one mistake or one trauma or one twist of fate could divert its direction and send it rushing downhill along some unexpected and destructive course? The question haunted Phoebe, particularly now that her own terrible family secret had been revealed.

But this was not some case study in a file on Diana's desk. It was personal. And even though Phoebe knew she did not have the power to change a single moment of what had transpired twenty years ago, she desperately wanted to find some answers.

What set the pattern in motion in the first place? Was there a key, some single pivotal event that governed everything that came afterward? And if there was, how could she possibly find it?

Phoebe pulled her legs up to her chest and rested her head on her knees. Hot tears leaked out and soaked into her jeans. Who could she talk to about this? A fleeting thought of Jake passed through her mind, followed by images of Krista's brilliant smile and Naomi's compassionate eyes. But no. She couldn't—wouldn't—reveal this horrible secret to them. What would they think of her? She had spent a lifetime protecting herself from rejection, drawing strength from her own sheer determination. And now, when the stakes were highest, she wasn't about to risk opening herself up to someone who could turn and walk away.

What she needed was *family*. Someone who had lived in the midst of the situation. Someone who could understand it from the inside.

A lump formed in Phoebe's throat, and she tried in vain to swallow it down. All the long-buried emotions pushed their way to the surface, and suddenly she was once more a tiny child cast adrift in a large and dangerous world. She longed for a Father who would comfort and protect her, for a Mother who would listen and understand. But God had abandoned and betrayed her just as surely as her biological father had. She wasn't inclined to go groveling to such a God to ask for anything now.

An image came to her mind—of herself, weary and travel-worn, turning a bend in the road and seeing Gram's house in the distance, high up on a hill. *Home.* And on the covered porch, peering into the setting sun, a small, wrinkled, gray-haired woman. Her grandmother. Waiting. Watching. Believing.

But Gram had lied to her, deceived her.

Phoebe had no family, at least none that she could trust. And even if there were someone she could connect with, how could it possibly help? Human beings were so pathetically limited. All Phoebe could see was what was right in front of her. Only this tiny slice of time, this present moment. She couldn't know the past, or the future. No one could.

There was no welcome for this prodigal. No word of safety or acceptance. Just the rain dripping from the eaves and splashing against the windowpane.

~

A crashing sound startled her awake. Phoebe raised her head and forced her eyes open. She had dozed off in the chair with one leg tucked under her.

What was the source of that noise? She looked around and saw Scooter with his back to her, perched on the third shelf of one of the bookcases. His hind end hung off the edge, and his tail twitched madly. Below him, on the floor, half a dozen books were scattered across the rug. He had one paw in behind the remaining books and was letting out that low, growling meow that signaled the presence of some potential prey.

"Scooter, get down!" Phoebe commanded.

He paid her no mind. Phoebe sincerely hoped he didn't have a mouse trapped back there. She wasn't afraid of mice, but she preferred not to have them in the house, and she didn't particularly want the job of having to dispose of one.

The cat continued to paw at the back of the bookcase, knocking off several more volumes in the process. With a sigh, Phoebe got up and forcibly removed Scooter from the shelf, setting him down among the fallen books. She leaned her ear close to the bookcase and listened. No scuttling sounds. Then she heard it: a high-pitched *chirrup*.

"Good grief, Scooter, it's just a cricket. Hardly worth all this bother."

He jumped up onto the library table and stalked back and forth, glaring at her. "Yeowww," he mewed.

Phoebe knew that sound. It meant, *You've taken away my plaything, and I'm not happy about it.*

Scooter continued to yell at her while she picked up the books and began to replace them on the shelf. "I know, you're mad at me," she said. "Well, I'm not too thrilled with you, either. You could at least have the decency to clean up your own messes."

Just as she leaned down for the last few volumes, Scooter jumped from the table, flicked his tail in Phoebe's face, and settled himself directly on top of a thick, battered book.

"Move," she said.

He didn't budge. He simply slit his golden eyes at her and flattened his ears. "Yeowww."

Phoebe sat down on the floor next to him. "Come on, let me have it." She pushed him aside—no mean feat, considering his twenty-pound physique—and picked up the book.

"What is this?"

Scooter came over to have a look. Apparently he had forgiven her for scaring away his cricket, for now he sidled up against her, purring and rubbing his cheek against the edges of the cover.

She wagged a warning finger at him. "No, it's not yours." Phoebe rubbed his ears, then turned back to the book. It was very old, its covers warped, its pages yellowed and brittle. The bowed binding, a faded green, had the words *Happy School Days: A Memory Book* embossed in gold on the front.

Phoebe had never seen anything like it. It was a bound book in a standard size—about nine by six, she estimated, but it was more like a scrapbook than anything else. Several photographs had dislodged in the fall and stuck out at odd angles. Phoebe pulled one loose and peered at it. Two young women, their arms linked together, beaming sepia-toned smiles from under bell-shaped cloche hats.

Phoebe regarded the photograph with detached interest. The twenties. Complete with bobbed hair, flouncy flapper skirts, and long swinging beads.

But whose book was it? Not Gram's, surely. She was almost eighty now, which meant she had been born in 1921. She had been a very small child—maybe even a baby—when these photographs were taken.

Phoebe turned back the front cover. On the inside, in a neat, concise hand, her answer was written. The ink was faded, but there could be no mistake.

Miss Phoebe Lange
1927

For the second time that morning, the world shifted beneath her. "It . . . it has my name in it," she said aloud.

Scooter responded with a curious "Roww?" and looked up at Phoebe.

Phoebe opened the book at random and found it filled with calling cards and old brown newspaper clippings and pictures of young women in knee-length flounced dresses and young men leaning rakishly against Model T Fords.

One photo in particular caught her attention—an attractive girl with short, curly hair and a wide, toothy smile. She was wearing a white sailor-style dress, and striking a pose with one hand on her hip and the other arm around a handsome fellow in a dapper three-piece suit. The handwritten caption read "Phoebe and Her Man."

Phoebe's breath caught in her throat. She could have been looking into a mirror, the resemblance was so strong. Her mind reeled, and the sense of disconnection from herself grew stronger. Seventy-five years ago, someone else had carried her name. Another Phoebe Lange.

Phoebe reached down to stroke Scooter's fur. Her hand was trembling. "I suppose I *must* have been named for her," she said. "But why didn't anyone ever tell me? I wonder what she was like."

She flipped forward and the Memory Book fell open to a page bearing the header "Favorite Teachers." A stern-faced woman stared back at her from a small photograph glued in the upper right-hand corner.

Dear Phoebe, a precise hand had written, *Congratulations upon your graduation, and most especially upon being chosen as valedictorian. I have every confidence that the brightest of futures lies before you. But always remember what you learned in my history class: "Those who forget the past are destined to repeat it." The past is the key to the future. Learn from yesterday, and your tomorrows will be marked by wisdom. With all good wishes, Iris Bellwether.*

Phoebe's eyes lingered on the words. An odd thrill went through her, as if she had just stepped through a portal and gone back in time. "The past," she whispered. "The past is the key to the future."

She wasn't sure exactly what that meant, but she intended to find out.

Beginning with everything she could learn about the original Phoebe Lange.

5

Unanswered Questions

Despite the emotional trauma of the morning—or perhaps because of it—Phoebe found that she was hungry. After she finished tidying up the bookshelves, she checked to make sure Gram was sleeping, then went down to the kitchen to make herself some lunch. Armed with a sandwich, chips, a bag of cookies, and a can of diet soda, she returned to the library—and the Memory Book.

The book seemed to call to her, almost as if it had a voice of its own. She cradled it in her hands, feeling the bowed binding, fingering the pages filled with memorabilia. When she opened it again, the nostalgic scent of ink and old paper filled her nostrils.

Nearly seventy-five years ago, a young woman bearing her name had put this book together, chronicling everything that held significance in her life. Photographs of friends. Tally cards from a bridge game. A playbill from the class drama. Birthday cards.

Party invitations. Place cards. Ticket stubs from the Majestic Theater—balcony level, Section E, Row R, Seats 4 and 5—for the opening of the silent version of *Ben-Hur*. Memories of special times. All clues to the personality and character of a woman now dead, who had carried Phoebe's name.

A shared name. What else, Phoebe wondered, did she and the original Phoebe Lange have in common? Shared genes, perhaps? Some thread that wound through time to bind them together?

She sipped at the diet soda, took a bite of the sandwich, and opened the Memory Book. There, on the inside front cover, was a bookplate bearing the handwritten name that had so startled her:

> *Miss Phoebe Lange*
> *Asheville, North Carolina*
> *1927*

She flipped through the first few pages. Class colors: Rose and Silver. Class Motto: *Carpe Diem*. Class Song: "Someone to Watch Over Me."

"Now we're getting to the good stuff," Phoebe murmured to herself as she turned the page and began a section entitled "My Schoolmates." Each page bore a photograph or two and a hand-written note, much the way students today had their yearbooks signed by friends and acquaintances. There were a good many of the "Don't forget me; I'll always remember you" variety of autographs. But to Phoebe's mind, the interesting ones were the messages from the original Phoebe Lange's closest friends.

Dearest Phoebe, a girl named Ethyle Taylor Sharp had written, *I've been so fortunate to have you for my best friend. You've taught me many things—most importantly, how to be honest with myself and others. I have you to thank for helping me reconcile with my mother. I will never forget you, and will always thank God for you.*

Albert Perkins, apparently the class clown, composed an original poem for the occasion:

> *I knew a girl named Phoebe,*
> *She was the cat's meow,*
> *And when she met her true love,*
> *She purred and purred, and how!*
> *Her true love fed her tuna pie*
> *And stroked her on the chin,*
> *And promised he would take her with him*
> *Everywhere he went.*

Another girlfriend, Mildred Craig, penned this note: *Phoebe, We've been best friends since the third grade, and know everything about each other. Everything. You've been my rock, and I will forever be grateful to you for loving me just as I am.*

The entries made Phoebe curious and struck her with a kind of awe. What kind of person was this Miss Phoebe, to generate such loyalty and devotion? And who was the mysterious "true love" who, according to Albert Perkins, had already promised to "take her with him everywhere he went"?

Phoebe flipped a few more pages and found what she was looking for.

My darling Phoebe,

Even tho' I graduated last year and am not part of your class, I am honored to write a few words in your book. Remember me as the man whose world was changed forever because of your love. Because of you, I see the beauty around me in new ways and can embrace it with my whole heart. My life is so much richer because of you. Through you I have learned to be myself and become the man I was created to be. I am your Sheik, and you are my Sheba, my mystery woman, my love. I give myself to you, heart and soul, forever.

J. B.

She stared uncomprehendingly at the words, *You are my mystery woman,* and the signature, *J. B.* How could it be? Miss Phoebe, nearly eight decades earlier, in love with a man who called her his "mystery woman" and had the same initials as her own fiancé, Jake Bartlett? Impossible.

But apparently it *was* possible. The next page was devoted to a larger photo of the two of them, arms around each other, perched on the running board of a Model T Roadster. The caption, clipped from a newspaper, read "A Rattlin' Romance" in bold print underneath. Handwritten in the margins were the names "Phoebe" and "Jonathan" with arrows drawn to the tops of their heads.

Phoebe hadn't realized she was holding her breath until she exhaled suddenly and gasped for oxygen. Jonathan. Not Jake. And Miss Phoebe's beau looked nothing like her own fiancé back in Atlanta. Jonathan wore suits and a felt fedora, and in nearly every picture he had his head cocked jauntily to one side as if to say, "I've got the goods." Still, the other parallels were unsettling.

"It's just a coincidence," she repeated. "An unbelievable coincidence." But the hairs on the back of her neck prickled nevertheless.

All afternoon as the rain drizzled, Phoebe sat in the chair next to the window and paged through Miss Phoebe's Memory Book. After her first random foray into the book, she started over more systematically. One page at a time, she began to piece together information about the unknown woman who shared her name.

Miss Phoebe had a large group of loving and supportive friends, especially the dapper young Jonathan and two girlfriends in particular, Ethyle and Mildred. Everyone liked her immensely, and, given the many entries, she must have been a strong leader among her peers and a good student. She had played the lead female role in the class play, a "gay little three-act suite" entitled *Tea Toper Tavern*. She wrote a column for the newspaper called "School Notes," and, as Iris Bellwether had indicated, had been named valedictorian of her graduating class.

Phoebe sorted through page after page of reminiscences and newspaper clippings that reported on the social events of the season. One in particular caught Phoebe's eye—a description of Miss Phoebe's eighteenth birthday party:

Miss Phoebe Lange entertained friends at her home on Saturday with three tables of bridge and high tea in honor of her eighteenth birthday. Miss Fern Perkins received the prize for high score. Following a most pleasant afternoon, the hostess served delicious refreshments, including finger sandwiches, candlestick salad, cranberry punch, coffee, ice cream, and chocolate layer cake. Guests in attendance were Misses Ernestine Wyler, Maureen Lester, Roena Cooley, Fern Perkins, Bessie Cruse, Savannah Wickmaster, Lorette Gamble, Ethyle Taylor Sharp, Mildred Craig, Veletha Hemmings, and Leontine Minor.

Other articles stood out, too. There was a lengthy movie review of the *Ben-Hur* premiere, entitled "World's Greatest Show." A notice about a junior-senior banquet, complete with the color scheme for the celebration, a menu list, and a full program of the speeches and music planned for the occasion. An advertisement for a photographic studio, claiming, "If there is beauty, we take it; if none, we make it."

Phoebe read on, discovering, of all unexpected things, an article about the organization of a girls' basketball team. One of Miss Phoebe's "School Notes" columns favored one particular alumnus by the name of Jonathan Barksdale—undoubtedly the one true love, Jonathan B. There was a handwritten "Class History," in couplets, obviously intended to incorporate the names of all the graduating seniors. And, pasted on a page all its own, a graduation invitation.

> *The Senior Class*
>
> *announces its*
>
> *Commencement Exercises*
>
> *Friday, May thirteenth*
>
> 1927
>
> 8:00 P.M.

It was all very interesting, and yet Phoebe felt a yearning rise up within her. This 1920s version of Phoebe Lange seemed to have everything she herself had always longed for—a genuinely happy life, friends who were loyal and devoted to her, a "true love" who adored her.

She supposed that outwardly she herself appeared to possess

these things, except that in Phoebe's world, they seemed shallow and superficial. This elder Phoebe had found some secret to authentic relationships, connections based not on an image she had created, but on reality. A stability based on honesty and truth.

Phoebe bit her lip and tried to rein in her thoughts. She was probably just projecting her own desires onto Miss Phoebe's life. This morning's revelations had dealt a crushing blow to her sense of self, and it was no doubt natural to look to someone else to help put the pieces back in place. But despite her rationalizations, Phoebe couldn't shake the sensation that she and this older Phoebe Lange were connected by more than a name and a few coincidences. She wanted to know more about this woman, more than the bits and pieces the Memory Book could communicate.

She closed the book, keeping her finger inside to hold her place, and stared pensively out the window, trying to identify the emotions that churned within her. Curiosity, certainly. But more than that. Longing. Envy, even.

That was it. She was envious of what Miss Phoebe Lange seemed to possess—the ability to let other people in, to have friends and loved ones from whom she kept no secrets. Yet Phoebe had always valued her independence. Since childhood she had always turned inward to work out her pains and struggles, and felt a sense of pride at the idea that she needed no one. Even as an adult, professing her love for Jake and her friendship with Krista and Naomi, she had held something back, unwilling to be completely vulnerable. Now, suddenly, she had begun to realize how very lonely self-sufficiency could be.

Beyond the windowpane she could see nothing but gray clouds and incessant rain. *The past,* history teacher Iris Bellwether had written, *is the key to the future.* Phoebe's own past had taken a dark and difficult turn today. Could Miss Phoebe's life have something to teach her, some hidden truth that might prove a catalyst to Phoebe's understanding of her own situation?

Phoebe shook her head. She didn't know how that could be possible. She didn't even know if she was related to the earlier Phoebe Lange. And yet, deep inside, she couldn't free herself from the eerie feeling that there was a connection between the two of them that went deeper than coincidence.

She was still watching the rain when she heard a faint "Mmwow" and felt twenty pounds of cat land squarely in her lap. The Memory Book slid off onto the floor at her feet, and Scooter, demanding attention in typical cat fashion, began kneading at her stomach with his front paws.

"Hey, buddy," she murmured, scratching him under the chin. He rolled over onto his back to have his belly rubbed. "You're just not getting enough attention these days, are you?" He stretched out his front legs, revealing the small patches of white fur underneath his armpits, and purred.

Phoebe retrieved a cookie from the bag on the end table and offered the last bit of leftover cheese from her sandwich to Scooter. He sat up on her lap and accepted it with detached delicacy, then with a final affectionate rub against her hand, jumped down and walked toward the door, his tail swaying back and forth like a sapling in the wind.

When the cat waved his final good-bye and exited the library, Phoebe turned her thoughts back to the Memory Book and all her unanswered questions. She found her place in the book and continued to page through. A few more pages of memorabilia, mostly centered around the upcoming graduation celebration, and then—

Nothing. The Memory Book ended abruptly. For a minute or two Phoebe kept turning, then sat back in the chair and frowned at the brittle, blank pages. Impossible. It couldn't just stop like that.

She flipped through every remaining page—a dozen or more, all blank—until she came to the back cover. There was nothing else.

Phoebe shut her eyes and sighed heavily. The situation reminded her of an archaeological dig she had seen once on PBS—the excavation of a city buried for centuries. When the archaeologists got down to ground level, they discovered plates and goblets and remains of food still on the table, as if some cataclysmic event had interrupted the evening meal. But not a sign of the inhabitants. It was as if they had simply vanished without a trace.

In frustration, she snapped the book shut and turned it face-down on her lap.

And then she saw it. The corner of a photograph, sticking out at an angle. Gingerly she lifted up the stiff back cover. The final page of the Memory Book had stuck to the inside cover, and a small picture was lodged in between.

Phoebe inserted her finger between the page and the back facing and pried gently. The two pages held fast, but the photograph fell out into her lap.

It was different from the other photos in the book—not a posed class picture, or a candid shot with friends mugging for the camera. This was a picture of a young woman standing on the broad front porch of a big house, her right arm wrapped protectively around a small boy. The boy, dressed in knickers with suspenders and a collarless white shirt, pressed against her, his eyes wide and dark, his hair cut in straight bangs across his forehead.

The young woman was obviously Miss Phoebe. But who was the child?

Phoebe looked closer, and recognition sizzled through her like an electric shock. The porch. The front door, half-hidden behind the little boy's head. The carved lintel. This was Gram's house. Her house.

She turned the photograph over. On the back were written the words:

Phoebe, age 18, with Little Brother Lewis, age 6

Phoebe's stomach lurched. Lewis.

Lewis Lange. Gram's husband. The grandfather she had never known, but whose actions had profoundly affected her own life.

What had her grandmother said about Lewis? *"He suffered a great deal . . . lost his mother when he was very young . . . his older sister cared for him . . ."*

Here was the connection she had been looking for. This wasn't a coincidence, a fluke. Miss Phoebe Lange was not some distant shirttail relative who just happened to have the same name. She was Phoebe's great-aunt.

Phoebe turned the photograph back over and scrutinized it. The child clearly adored his big sister. Rather than standing apart from her or grimacing at the affectionate touch, as little boys were wont to do, he stood as near to her as he could possibly get, leaning into the embrace.

The poor boy's mother had died. Phoebe knew all too well what a loss of that magnitude could do to a child's psyche. And yet he was obviously loved and cared for, a factor that, while not making up for the loss of a mother, should have gone a long way in enabling him to grow up as a relatively healthy and compassionate person.

How then had this innocent child, this sweet-looking little boy, grown into a man who browbeat and threatened her grandmother? A man who, by example, had taught his own son that dominating women, even to the point of deadly force, was acceptable behavior?

Phoebe begged for answers, for clarity. And yet every time an answer seemed to present itself, it was accompanied by a hundred more questions, each more baffling than the last.

She shut her eyes, and when she opened them again, she

found herself looking down at the final page of the Memory Book. Something else was stuck between the last page and the back cover. Her fingers identified a flat lump against the rigid binding of the book, but she couldn't seem to pry the page loose and didn't want to tear it.

With the Memory Book in hand, she went to the library table and rummaged in the single flat drawer until she came up with a thin brass letter opener. Carefully, so as not to damage the book or its contents, she slid the tip of the opener into a small opening at one corner and worked it around the outside edges. At last the final page came free, and a vellum card slipped out onto the table.

It was a heavy-stock card, like the ones used as calling cards, but larger, and only slightly rectangular—not quite five by seven. The paper, once white, had aged to the color of cream cheese, and a wide black border surrounded the printing.

In Memoriam
Phoebe Elizabeth Lange
Born
March 3, 1909
Died
May 13, 1927
Her memory will live in
our hearts forever.

6

In Memoriam

Phoebe gazed at the card, her mind refusing to comprehend what her eyes saw. The formal white vellum, now yellowed with age. The wide black border. The name, Phoebe Elizabeth Lange. And the words that rang with an ominous finality: *In Memoriam*.

She stared, disbelieving, until the black words and border imprinted themselves upon her retina, so that even when she looked away she still saw the card, white against black, like a photographic negative. A lump formed in her throat and tears stung her eyes.

Phoebe struggled to evaluate her emotional response. She felt as if she had just learned of the unexpected death of a dear friend. And yet it didn't feel like a friend's death. It felt like her own. Like Ebenezer Scrooge getting that first shrouded glimpse of his own headstone. She fought against the smothering weight on her soul, the claustrophobia of her own mortality, the crushing fear of dying before she had a chance to live.

Her rational mind, of course, had known that Great-Aunt Phoebe had to be dead. But somehow she had imagined her life differently—graduating from high school, maybe going on to college, marrying her true love, Jonathan, living happily ever after until a peaceful death took her in ripe old age. Not dead at eighteen.

Eighteen.

Something about the memorial card nagged at Phoebe's mind, and she looked at it again. Born March 3, 1909. Died May 13, 1927.

She grabbed up the Memory Book and began searching frantically through its pages until she found what she was looking for. The commencement invitation.

Her eyes flitted back and forth from the invitation to the memorial card. Friday, May 13, 1927.

Great-Aunt Phoebe's life had ended on graduation night.

Gram held the Memory Book in both hands and blinked hard as her eyes misted over. "I had no idea this still existed," she said. "Where did you find it?"

"In the library. Scooter knocked some books off a shelf going after a cricket." Phoebe pulled a chair up next to the bed and sat down. "You have to tell me what you know about this Phoebe Lange," she said. "It's important."

"Why is this so vital to you, child?"

Phoebe hesitated. She couldn't say, *I need answers about my father, my family, myself.* She couldn't say, *I can't talk to you because you lied to me.* And so she said, "I'm not sure. I just feel—I don't know, *compelled* to find out about her. I was named for her?"

Gram nodded. "Your grandfather insisted on it. He loved his sister very much."

"Everyone did, if the photos and inscriptions in the Memory Book are any indication. What did Grandpa Lewis say about her, Gram? Tell me everything."

Her grandmother shook her head. "He rarely spoke her name, except for the day you were born. He was already quite ill by that time, and even though his relationship with your father had often been rocky and difficult, your mother couldn't find it in her heart to refuse him. I'll tell you what I know, but it isn't much."

Phoebe leaned forward, suppressing the urge to say, *Tell me the truth this time.* "I'm listening."

"Your great-aunt Phoebe was not quite twelve years old when Lewis was born. Their mother died shortly after giving birth, and Phoebe took on the job of raising her little brother."

"So she was more like a mother than a sister to him."

"I suppose so."

"Where was their father in all this? My great-grandfather?"

"I don't know. Lewis didn't speak of him, either, except to say that they didn't get along very well."

Phoebe held up the memorial card and placed it on the bed next to the Memory Book. "She died on May 13, 1927. Graduation night. Do you know what happened?"

Gram's eyes clouded over. "That much I do know—although not from Lewis but from other friends and relatives. Phoebe died in a motorcar accident—a terrible crash. Drove into the side of a mountain very late at night. According to those who told me about it, Phoebe's father, Gerald, reacted very strangely to her death. He spurned any attempts at consolation and didn't even attend the funeral. Afterwards, he sealed up her room, left it exactly the way it was the day she died, and forbade anyone to talk about her, even so much as to utter her name in his presence."

"Which room?" Even as she asked the question, Phoebe was certain she knew the answer.

"The tower bedroom. Your room."

Phoebe felt a chill run through her veins. First her father, now this. Her mind spun off onto a thousand tangents, and when she came back to the present, her grandmother was still speaking.

"But Lewis never found it," she was saying.

Phoebe forced herself back to the conversation. "Sorry, Gram. Could you repeat that?"

"Lewis never found it," her grandmother repeated.

"Found what?"

"The diary. His sister had kept a diary, a journal of sorts. Once when he was very small, he walked into her room and saw her writing in it. She put it away immediately, but he didn't know where she kept it. He was always obsessed with the idea of discovering it. Even very late in his life he would go off on a tear every now and then, searching for it. But she must have had it with her in the car the night she died, and if she did, it was lost forever. At any rate, he never found it."

Phoebe sat quietly for a minute or two, trying to take in all her grandmother had told her. "Is that all?" she asked at last.

"I've told you everything I know. As I said, Lewis rarely talked about her. Yet he clearly loved her." She paused, and her voice caught in her throat. "Once, when I was young, I foolishly thought otherwise, but now I suspect she was the only person he ever truly loved."

Phoebe stood behind the open door of the library, carefully scanning the bookshelf in front of her. She didn't really expect to find Great-Aunt Phoebe's diary in full view, given what Gram had told her about the way her great-aunt carefully concealed it from prying eyes. To be honest, she had little hope of finding it anywhere. After all, Grandpa Lewis had never managed to unearth it. But still she felt compelled to look, and she didn't know where else to start.

And what if by some miracle she found it? Under ordinary

circumstances she would not even consider reading someone else's private journal. It would be a violation of trust, an intrusion.

But these were no ordinary circumstances. For one thing, Great-Aunt Phoebe was no longer living. Her diary had been hidden untouched for ages, perhaps three-quarters of a century. And more importantly, Phoebe believed—or at least hoped—that it might offer some resolution to the questions that tormented her. If not answers, then clues. Hints. Something that would help her impose a bit of order upon the chaos of confusion that enveloped her. Surely her great-aunt would understand that need.

Please, she begged silently. *Please let me find it.*

A noise behind her startled her, and she turned to see Hargraves standing in the doorway.

"You shouldn't sneak up on a person like that!" Phoebe blurted out. "You scared me."

"Wasn't sneaking," Hargraves answered curtly. "I thought, since you made it clear you weren't a *guest,* it was about time you pulled your weight around here." She shifted her frame and looked pointedly at her wristwatch.

The clock on the mantelpiece chimed five. "Dinnertime already?" Phoebe said. "I didn't realize it was so late. I'll . . . of course I'll help."

Hargraves didn't budge. "What are you doing?"

"Just . . . just looking. At the books," Phoebe said.

"Humph," said the nurse. She turned on her heel and disappeared.

By the time Phoebe got down the stairs, Hargraves was already banging pots and pans. *The woman is right,* she thought as she passed through the living room on her way to the kitchen, *I should be helping out more.* The entire house needed to be cleaned and the bathrooms scrubbed. Her grandmother had always been, if not an immaculate housekeeper, at least a competent one, and she had taught Phoebe that livable and littered were not synonymous.

A twinge of guilt nagged at her. She had been so absorbed with her own personal dilemmas and Great-Aunt Phoebe's Memory Book that she hadn't given more than a passing thought to anything else all day.

After dinner, Phoebe vowed to herself, she would dust and vacuum and get rid of the layers of Scooter's hair and the little dust kittens that had collected in the corners. She didn't have the time or the energy for a thorough spring cleaning, but she could at least make herself useful and put the place back into some semblance of order. And in the meantime, she would do everything she could to help Hargraves with the cooking and with Gram's care.

But Phoebe's resolve was almost immediately diverted by the ringing of the doorbell.

"I'll get it!" she called in the direction of the kitchen. She swung open the heavy front door to reveal a teenage boy in blue jeans, his face completely obscured by an enormous bank of red roses and white baby's-breath.

"Delivery for Phoebe Lange."

"That's me."

He thrust the flower vase into Phoebe's arms and held out a clipboard. "Sign here." He pointed to a blank space on the form.

With some difficulty, Phoebe scrawled her name as she balanced the flowers. "Thank you."

The delivery boy gave no indication that he intended to move. A tip. Of course, he expected a tip. But Phoebe's purse was upstairs, and she certainly wasn't going to ask Hargraves for any money. She shook her head. "I'm sorry, I—"

"Whatever. Have a nice day." He shrugged his shoulders and ambled back to the van.

Phoebe closed the door with her foot and took the flowers into the living room. She set the vase on a sideboard and fished for the card, which read: *For my mystery woman. Hope all is well. Am praying for you and holding you close to my heart. Love, J. B.*

She gazed at the card and fingered the velvety petals of one of the roses. Two dozen of them, not bright red but a deep burgundy color. They sent out the most heavenly fragrance into the musty, closed-up room. Phoebe stifled back a rush of annoyance. She ought to be flattered, but instead she found herself irritated. *For my mystery woman.* Very funny.

You wouldn't be sending flowers if you knew the mystery behind the woman, Phoebe thought acidly. *You'd be out the door before these roses had a chance to wilt.*

But Jake wasn't to blame, she knew. It was a nice gesture, even though a couple dozen roses—or a hundred dozen—couldn't begin to alleviate the pain and confusion she had endured this day. He didn't know what she had learned about her mother's death, about her father's character, about her grandfather's life.

And she wasn't about to tell him, either. He might love her now, but it was an empty promise, given in ignorance. A sweet sentiment, nothing more. She wouldn't hold him to it. As soon as she got back to Atlanta and could sit with him face to face, she would break off their engagement. She wouldn't tell him why, of course. She couldn't. And even though breaking up with him would hurt him, it wouldn't hurt nearly as much as knowing the truth about the family he was inheriting by marrying her. A quick, clean ending would be the best thing for both of them. A surgical cut, which would heal with a minimum of scarring.

No, she wouldn't tell him. He would insist on talking everything out, on probing into the depths of her soul. And once the truth was out, he would still marry her even if he no longer wanted to. He would be noble, and she didn't think she could stand the idea of being the object of someone else's charity. There were some problems you just didn't talk out. You buried them, ignored them. And if they clawed their way to the light again, you simply threw more dirt on top and walked away.

Hargraves came out of the kitchen and stood in the middle of the dining room. "Who was at the door?" She caught a glimpse of the flowers and came over to stand next to Phoebe. "Roses. They're beautiful. From an admirer, I take it?"

Phoebe stared at her. Was it possible the Battle-axe really did have a heart buried under that starched white uniform? "From my fiancé, Jake," Phoebe muttered.

"Ah." The nurse's lips twitched as if she were trying on a smile—or attempting to suppress one. "Had a fight, did you?"

"Not a fight. I think he's just—well, trying to make a connection."

The smile broke through, softening the hard lines of Hargraves's angular face. "Connection like that could cause some serious sparks."

Phoebe watched, amazed at the transformation of Hargraves's countenance. Maybe Gram was right. Maybe there was a good soul buried beneath that brusque exterior. But even so, Phoebe wasn't inclined to expose her emotions to the woman.

"I didn't mean to cloister myself away all day," Phoebe said. "I just got distracted. After dinner, I'm going to do some cleaning down here, if you don't think the noise of the vacuum will disturb Gram too much."

Hargraves regarded her with an expression that almost bordered on respect. "Your grandmother would appreciate that, I believe. Now, you want to help with dinner?"

Phoebe grinned. "Absolutely." She pulled one long-stemmed rose out of the arrangement. "Maybe we could find a bud vase and put this on Gram's tray."

Hargraves motioned with her head, indicating that Phoebe should follow, and turned back toward the kitchen. But before Phoebe took two steps, the telephone began to ring. "I'll answer it."

She handed the rosebud to the nurse and picked up the receiver. "Lange residence."

"Did you get the flowers?" a male voice asked.

"Yes, they just arrived." Phoebe bit the inside of her jaw and tried to infuse a modicum of enthusiasm into her voice. "They're beautiful, Jake. Thank you so much."

"You're welcome. I wanted you to know I was thinking about you."

"You didn't have to send fifty dollars' worth of roses to say it."

"Sometimes a tangible reminder is helpful."

"That's very sweet," Phoebe said. She let out a pent-up breath and changed the subject. "How are you doing?"

"Work's going fine. I got a big case today, a complex one involving a surrogate mother and the custody of the child she gave birth to. It's the kind of case that usually doesn't go to a new associate. I guess that means the partners really believe in me."

"That's nice."

She could almost hear him frowning through the telephone lines. "Is something wrong?" he asked.

Phoebe hesitated. "No. I'm just tired."

"I miss you. How's your grandmother?"

"A little better, I think. The pneumonia itself wears her out, and the antibiotics make her tired as well. But she's getting stronger." Dead air stretched between them, and she fought to fill it. "Thanks for asking. The nurse and I are just about to fix her dinner."

"I won't keep you, then. Give Gram my love." His voice was gentle, his tone compassionate. "Are you getting any rest?"

"I didn't sleep well last night, and I've got a lot of work to do this evening—cleaning the house, that sort of thing. Scrubbing toilets isn't exactly my favorite job, but everything has been let go since Gram got sick."

He chuckled—an odd, strangled sound over the telephone lines. "It's a dirty job—"

"But somebody has to do it," she finished automatically.

"When we get married," he said, "I'll clean the toilets. Or we'll hire someone to come in once a week. You'll never have to scrub a bathroom again."

There it was—the *M* word again. Phoebe gazed at the massive arrangement of roses. For a split second she almost decided to take the risk and pour it all out to him—what she had learned about her mother's death, the terrible revelation about her father, everything. To tell him about finding the Memory Book, and about Great-Aunt Phoebe's missing diary, and about all the unanswered questions about the past and herself that plagued her. To find out whether he really would love her if he knew about her insecurities, her fear. But she hesitated, and the inclination passed as quickly as it had come. Some things couldn't be cured with a Band-Aid, a kiss, and a pat on the head.

"Phoebe, are you still there?"

"Yes, I'm here." She exhaled heavily. "But I need to go help with dinner."

"All right. Shall I call you tomorrow night?"

"OK. Thanks again for the flowers, Jake," she said. "It was so thoughtful."

"Well, I'm a thoughtful guy." He laughed. "Remember that when we're married and I ignore you because I'm obsessed with a case."

"Sure."

There was a pause while static crackled on the line. "I love you, sweetheart."

"I love you, too." She said it hurriedly, then hung up the receiver before he could get in another word.

7

The Secret Place

It was nearly eleven by the time Phoebe completed the cleaning list she had set for herself. After dinner, which she shared with her grandmother in her room, she had insisted that Hargraves go rest or read or watch TV or whatever she did to relax. With the nurse out of the way, Phoebe washed the dishes and cleaned the kitchen from top to bottom. She scrubbed both bathrooms thoroughly, then tackled the dust, cat hair, and cobwebs in the living and dining rooms. Scooter followed her from room to room, complaining loudly over the noise of the vacuum and trying to catch the dust rag as it moved around the wooden legs of the furniture.

"Don't you yell at me, you beast," Phoebe told him, shaking a huge wad of cat hair in his face. "You're the primary reason I have to do this."

He rubbed his face against her hand and strolled away.

Phoebe couldn't help laughing. She and Krista, a die-hard

dog person, had long engaged in a continuing debate about the relative merits of the two species. Like most dog owners, Krista disparaged cats for being indifferent to their owners' emotions. "Dogs understand everything their humans feel," she would insist. But now, as Phoebe watched Scooter lumbering across the room with his tail in the air, she couldn't help being convinced that cats understood everything their owners felt, too—they just didn't care.

She pushed back the draperies and opened the front windows. A cool evening breeze blew through the downstairs rooms, mixing that wonderful early-summer scent of blooming flowers and fresh-mown grass with the faint scent of lemon polish. Phoebe despised housecleaning, but she had to admit she liked seeing the immediate results from her labors. She might not be able to impose order upon the chaos in her mind and heart, but she could at least find a little satisfaction in setting Gram's house to rights.

Carrying a glass of iced tea out onto the porch, she settled herself in the swing and propped up her aching feet. Even here, on a city street in Asheville, tree frogs chirped their nightly chorus, bringing the country into the center of town. Their song worked its way into her heart, and she exhaled the day's tension on a sigh.

Strange, how even in the midst of the trauma of this day, she could still find a moment of tranquillity. There was something soothing and comforting about the mountains, as if the higher she went, the further removed she was from the day's troubles. The city motto of Asheville was *Altitude Affects Attitude,* and Phoebe had long known it was true. In Atlanta, her spirit was constantly assaulted by noise and hurry and stress. Traffic gridlocked, or flying along at eighty miles an hour. Horns honking. Sirens blaring. People everywhere, rushed and angry and impatient.

And she could never see the stars.

When she left Asheville and transferred to Emory, Phoebe hadn't counted on missing the stars so much. She had grown from girl to woman wishing on the first bright star at the top of the eastern ridges, watching as the rose-hued sky darkened to purple, then blue, then a black as soft and rich as velvet, spangled with a million diamonds. She had poured her dreams into the Big Dipper and hung her hopes on Orion's Belt. The stars had comforted her, made her feel safe, as if all the eyes of heaven were looking down upon her.

Five years she had been in Atlanta. Sixty long months of voluntary incarceration. Eighteen hundred nights of a sky that reflected back not the wonder of nature but the pale pink glow of human progress.

She had almost forgotten how dark the Blue Ridge nights were, and how bright the stars could be.

⌒

Stars. The stars were everywhere, cascading across a deep blue cosmos. Countless swirling nebulae, red giants, white dwarfs.

The glittering sash of the Milky Way cinching the waistline of the universe. Polaris, bright in the northern sky, winking at her, whispering her name. Calling to her: *Come home.*

But where was home? Phoebe thrashed in her bed, vaguely aware of reaching out toward something. Even in her dream, she could feel the longing, a vast, empty chasm inside her soul. Dark nothingness yearning to be filled. And there, on the top of the highest ridge, silhouetted like a black paper cutout against the infinitude of stars, a figure on the mountaintop. A woman—a girl, really. Waving her hand. Motioning for Phoebe to draw nearer.

Phoebe approached—flying, it seemed, on the wings of the night breeze. Effortlessly gliding closer and closer until she had almost reached the top of the ridge. Below, she could see the layers of valley and mountain folding in upon one another, sleeping giants embracing under a blanket of trees. Closer and closer she came until she floated directly in front of the woman on the mountaintop.

She could see the face now, pale in the dim starlight. The short wavy hair blown back by the wind. The dark eyes. The mouth that turned up slightly on one side. As if she were looking into a mirror, years ago. Her face.

"We are one," the voice murmured, barely a whisper on the chilled air. "Past and present and future. It is all a unity, all one. We are the same."

Then whatever force was holding her suspended above the mountains gave way, and Phoebe was falling, falling . . .

⁓

She jerked upright, breathing hard. The dream had been so real that she looked around her room in a daze, surprised to find herself alive and in her own bed in the tower room. Liquid light from a quarter moon poured like milk through the window-pane, splashing over the bedspread and dripping onto the hardwood floor.

Phoebe sat up and put her bare feet on the floorboards. Their firm coldness comforted her, brought her back to reality.

Still, she couldn't shake the feeling that the dream meant something. Her younger self, up on the mountaintop, saying— what was it? She racked her brain, trying to remember, trying to grab hold of the elusive images that seemed to dance just outside her reach. Something about past and present and future as a unity. *"We are one. We are the same."*

Then a thought occurred to her, an idea that chilled her more thoroughly than the night air coming through the open window or the cold floor under her feet. What if the girl she saw on the mountain was someone else? Not herself, but someone who looked remarkably like her?

Great-Aunt Phoebe.

She did not for a moment believe that her great-aunt had

actually come to her with a message from beyond. Speaking to the dead was the stuff of con artists and hustlers. This was different. It was a dream, and dreams were born out of the subconscious.

So what was her subconscious trying to tell her?

The answer came fully formed, sprung from her mind whole and entire: she had been right all along. Somehow Great-Aunt Phoebe held the key to her questions about her family, her past, her identity.

The conviction descended upon her in a rush, like the first precipitous drop in a roller coaster. Her stomach floated in midair for a moment, and then all the air went out of her lungs.

She had to find Great-Aunt Phoebe's diary.

But where? She had looked in the library and hadn't found it there. It might be stuck in a crevice behind some of the other books, as the Memory Book had been. But Grandpa Lewis had searched for it off and on his entire life, Gram said, and never found it.

The voice in the dream came back to her: *"We are one. We are the same."*

If she and Great-Aunt Phoebe were indeed that much alike, it stood to reason that she might be able to deduce where her great-aunt had hidden the diary. She let her gaze wander around the darkened tower room. *Her* room, at least since she grew old enough not to fear its shadows. And Great-Aunt Phoebe's as well.

The room, though spacious, was sparsely furnished. The bed, two nightstands, a couple of lamps. A dresser, empty except for the socks and underwear and jeans Phoebe had stashed in the top two drawers. A full-length cheval mirror, and a couple of small hooked rugs. An old platform rocker, its upholstery sun faded from pink to a washed-out shade of salmon. And against the opposite wall, the big oak armoire with its tall double doors.

The moon had shifted a bit and now lay in rectangular bars across the face of the freestanding wardrobe. Phoebe's eyes lingered on the carved oak doors. Its interior was lined with cedar. Phoebe could still recall the scent of it in her mind. What memories that smell brought back to her!

The armoire had been her thinking place. When she was a child and wanted to be completely alone and private, she would slip inside and shut the doors. The darkness and warmth enveloped her like a womb; the rich aroma from the cedar panels surrounded and comforted her. It had always been—

The hair on the back of her neck twitched as her mind finished the thought. *Her favorite hiding place.* Might it have been Great-Aunt Phoebe's hiding place, too?

Phoebe snapped on the lamp, squinting as the harsh bulb dispelled the shadows created by the softer moonlight. The clock on the bedside table read three-fifteen. She held her breath, listening.

On bare feet, she padded to the door and slipped out into the hall. A small night-light cast a faint glow down the hallway, but there was no sign of anyone being awake. Three rooms down, she could hear Hargraves sawing logs. She tiptoed in the other direction, toward Gram's room. Nothing was stirring.

Even Scooter, the night prowler, was curled up asleep on the rug in front of her grandmother's door, his rumbling purr a counter-point to the nurse's snores.

Phoebe went back to her room, shut the door, and sat on the bed, shivering. Now that she was out of bed, she was cold. She pulled on a sweatshirt over her pajamas and donned a pair of socks. After double-checking the rest of the drawers in the dresser—just to be sure—she went and stood in front of the oak wardrobe.

Gingerly she opened the right-hand door a crack and winced as it squeaked on its hinges. Unaccountably, her heart began to pound erratically, as if something were about to jump out at her. She could almost hear eerie music in the background, but it was only the roaring of her pulse in her ears.

Don't be ridiculous, she reprimanded herself. *This isn't an Alfred Hitchcock movie.* Still, the lateness of the hour and the quiet-ness of the house unnerved her. Summoning all her courage, she took a deep breath and flung the wardrobe wide open.

It was empty. Except for the clothes she had brought with her—one jacket, a couple of blouses, a pair of black trousers, and a navy suit, in case she needed to dress up—there was noth-ing inside.

Phoebe stifled her initial rush of disappointment. What had she expected? Great-Aunt Phoebe wouldn't have left her private diary just lying on the floor of the armoire where Grandpa Lewis—or anyone else—might find it.

She collected her clothes, laid them, hangers and all, on the bed, and then went back to examine the wardrobe more carefully. First she investigated the inside. All the cedar panels were in place, and there was no sign that anyone had tampered with any of them. The outside looked normal, too—no crevices big enough to hide anything in—and the piece was so heavy that it would have taken two strong men to move it away from the wall, so she assumed there was nothing attached to the back of it. She got down on her belly and looked underneath, where the heavy carved legs raised the armoire six inches above the floor. It was dark there, and she could see little. She felt around with both hands but came up only with cobwebs, a dead spider, and several little fur kittens, compliments of Scooter.

Disappointed, Phoebe struggled to her feet and sank into the rocking chair. She narrowed her eyes and stared at the wardrobe as if it might voluntarily give up its secrets under the searchlight of her gaze. It was very tall—nearly nine feet high—and crafted of fine-grain oak which had mellowed over the years to a deep honey color. The top curved upward in the center and was crowned by a molding that matched the carvings on the doors.

She had been so certain that she would find Great-Aunt Phoebe's diary in the armoire. But she had been over every inch of the piece. There was no place to hide anything outside, and the inside was flawless, all the cedar panels squarely joined and mitered, a perfect rectangle, about six feet wide and eight feet high. Nothing loose or warped or—

Phoebe's thoughts ground to a halt. A rectangle. The outside of the armoire was curved at the top, but the inside was rectangular.

She got up and went back to the wardrobe, peering inside at its cedar ceiling. Yes. It was, as she remembered, flat, rising about eighteen inches higher than the wooden dowel that served as a hanging rod.

She stepped back and craned her neck to look up. Visually, the front of the wardrobe was all of one piece, all the way up to the curved molding. But the outside seemed taller—nearly a foot taller, according to her estimate—than the inside.

Phoebe's heart began to accelerate. She looked around for something to stand on. There was only the rocking chair, not a very sturdy choice. But if she went downstairs to find a stepladder, she might wake somebody up.

She'd just have to be careful. She dragged the rocking chair over to one side of the wardrobe and balanced herself on the seat. From this vantage point she couldn't see over the top, but she could tell that the wardrobe was, essentially, a big box with a flat top. The carved molding that rose up in the front was a facade.

She stretched as far as she could and ran one hand behind the curved wood. Obviously no one ever dusted up here; she was probably stirring up dirt that had lain untouched for nearly a century. Or at least seventy-five years.

Then her hand touched something—a lump. A flat, squarish

lump, wedged under the very edge of the molding. Her fingers closed around it. The chair lurched under her shifting weight, and she braced herself against the edge of the wardrobe. With a trembling that shuddered throughout her body, she brought the treasure down.

It was a small book, perhaps five inches by seven inches, bound in a light-brown leather made soft through handling. One of its edges was a bit ragged, and it was filthy with the accumulated grime of decades, but otherwise it was in remarkably good shape.

Phoebe propped her left hand against the wardrobe for support and with the right swiped the book, front and back, across the sleeve of her sweatshirt. Then, balancing her weight to compensate for the swaying motion of the platform rocker, she took the book in both hands and opened it.

The face pages were a soft cream color, and there, inside the front cover, in the neat handwriting Phoebe had come to recognize so well, was an inscription that made her heart dance:

Property of Phoebe Elizabeth Lange

Private

8

The Diary

Phoebe found that she was trembling, but whether from cold or excitement she couldn't say. She laid the journal on the bedside table and spent a minute or two putting the room to rights—replacing the rocking chair, returning her clothes to the wardrobe.

But if she had hoped that the process of straightening the room might serve to calm her hammering heart, she was disappointed. The brief delay, those deliberate actions of moving the chair and rearranging the clothes, only heightened her anticipation of the revelation to come. Still, she wanted to give her undivided attention to the diary, and she couldn't focus surrounded by disarray.

She went to the bathroom, filled her water glass from the tap, straightened the bedding. When everything seemed in order, she crawled under the covers and held the book in her lap, caressing its leather cover with her hands.

Then, holding her breath, she opened it and began to read.

~

January 1, 1927

The New Year has come, and all day everyone has been talking about last night's party and formulating New Year's resolutions. And yet, with the turning of this page, I find myself with far more questions than resolutions.

This is my last year of high school—the final few months, people say, of innocent childhood. Why, then, do I feel as if my own childhood—and my innocence—ended years ago? Have I been simply playing the role of high school student when in truth my soul has aged before its time?

Part of my purpose in writing all this down is to find out. I am going to try to be honest with myself, here in this place where no prying eyes will ever see what I write.

Phoebe paused as a twinge of guilt shot through her. Great-Aunt Phoebe assumed—and rightfully so—that no one else would ever read these private thoughts. And under other circumstances, she would never have considered reading another person's journal. But the dream, those whispered words, *"We are one,"* left Phoebe with a sense of implicit permission, the feeling that somehow her great-aunt, now long dead, would want her to have the diary, would be pleased if something she had written helped her grandniece to find her way.

It was blatant rationalization, probably. But Phoebe pushed aside those feelings and read on.

When Mother died, everything changed. Father became sullen and withdrawn, began to drink heavily, and paid little attention either to Lewis or to me. Perhaps he simply had no idea what to do with an infant, or perhaps he no longer cared about anything— even his own life, even his own children. Whatever the case, I became an adult that day, in one sweeping trans-formation. I took Mother's place with Lewis and tended him as if he were my own.

That was six years ago. Six years when I should have been out playing with my friends, discovering boys, enjoying the carefree life of a child. Instead, I had a child—not a baby doll that could be played with or stored in a cupboard at will, but a living baby who demanded constant attention and care.

I cannot regret or be resentful of Lewis, certainly. I love him with all my heart and cannot imagine life without him. And perhaps—I hope, I pray—I have been good for him, too. But despite all that, I have to admit that I've lost something. Some sense of connec-tion to other people, some sense of who I am. On the surface, I seem to be at the center of everything—school, friends, my column for the newspaper, this budding friendship (could it be more?) with Jonathan Barksdale. And yet deep down, I feel isolated, as if I am standing on the outside looking in. As if I am different, somehow, from everyone else in a way that doesn't readily show.

And I wonder, do any of these people—my friends at school, Ethyle and Mildred, even Jonathan—have any idea what is on the inside? Do they know what makes me laugh or what makes me cry? Do they care about the real me or only about the image they see? And how can they truly care, when all they see is the image?

The first day's entry ended there, and Phoebe turned the book facedown in her lap. So there *were* more similarities between herself and her great-aunt than a name, a family resemblance, and a few shared genes! She closed her eyes and tried to reconcile the conflicting emotions that battered at her heart. Sadness for the pain and uncertainty Great-Aunt Phoebe had expressed. Hope for herself, that at last she had stumbled upon someone who was capable of understanding what she was going through. Regret that Great-Aunt Phoebe was no longer alive to talk with in person. And over all those feelings, like a sky full of threatening clouds, apprehension that even Great-Aunt Phoebe might not hold any answers for her.

But unless she read more of the diary, she would never find out.

January 2, 1927

After rereading yesterday's entry, I realized I did not even scratch the surface in trying to set forth the questions and struggles that swirl around in my mind and heart. Last fall Artemis Lodge at the paper told me that a good journalist must display two characteristics toward her subject: honesty and ruthlessness. I have already committed myself to honesty, although I was only "partially honest" with myself yesterday. Since my subject is myself, and my life, I will henceforth attempt a fuller confession and a more deliberate ruthlessness in getting to the truth.

The first truth is I am not quite certain why I am keeping this diary. The arrival of a New Year, certainly, tends to motivate a nostalgic kind of reassessment in most people—taking stock of the old year and determining to do better in the new. But this exercise in writing goes far deeper than that. As graduation looms on the horizon, I am facing a watershed moment in my life. What happens after I graduate? College, perhaps? A career in journalism—difficult, at best, for a woman? Marriage and a family?

Everyone around me seems to have certain expectations of me, but before I launch out into full adulthood, I believe it would be wise for me to come to grips with myself, to find out who I am and what I want out of life. And most importantly, to resolve some concerns in my life that cause me pain.

So let us face the problems head-on:

Father. Where my father is concerned, I tend to want to make excuses for him. He has endured so much personal tragedy—most specifically, the loss of Mother when Lewis was born. But if I am to be both honest and ruthless, I have to admit that I am angry with him, and have been for a long time. Not only because he robbed me of a large part of my childhood by abdicating my baby brother into my care, but because he has never, since Mother's death, offered me so much as a word of gratitude. Even the dogs get the crumbs that fall from the master's table.

Setting aside, for the moment, my need for a father who gives me love and appreciation, I must also admit that I am frightened of him—on my own account, but even more for Lewis's sake—especially when Father has been drinking. Now that my brother is growing up a little, Father shows him attention, but not the kind of attention he needs. I have seen the hateful *expression on Father's face when Lewis catches his eye, and I fear that Father blames Lewis for Mother's death. I have also heard Father disciplining Lewis behind closed doors—the kind of discipline imposed by the strap. Just last week, after we opened Christmas gifts, Father began shouting at Lewis because he showed more preference for my gift (a book of adventure stories) than for Father's (a child-sized air rifle).*

Lewis is a sweet, tender boy who loves to read and even enjoys helping me in the kitchen. He demonstrates his emotions readily. I am greatly warmed by his child-like love and devotion. But Father is determined to make him into a "man's man" and not let him "get soft," even if he has to beat the softness out of him with a belt. I fear Lewis may give in to Father's browbeating and change in order to please him—especially when I am no longer here to protect him.

Phoebe stared at the journal. These were not just words on a page—they were the handwriting on the wall. The answer to at least one of her questions.

Great-Aunt Phoebe had died only a few months after this entry had been written. She hadn't been there to protect Lewis from his father's influence. And so Lewis had grown up into a "man's man," a man who, like his father, expressed his anger and pain through an ironfisted rule over those less powerful than himself—his wife and son.

The son who grew up to become Phoebe's own father, the man who beat her mother to death.

And gentle, sweet six-year-old Lewis Lange had been the first of the dominoes to fall.

9

Pandora's Box

Distracted by thoughts of young Lewis and the connecting links between him and her own parents, Phoebe dozed off and awoke a few hours later just as the first rays of sunlight painted the tower room with a hazy pink wash. Great-Aunt Phoebe's diary still lay open facedown on the bed beside her.

She strained her ears and listened for a minute or two. The house was still quiet. The clock at her bedside read six-fifteen.

Phoebe got up and tiptoed across the hall to use the bathroom and brush her teeth. The door creaked on its hinges as it opened and shut, and she winced inwardly, hoping no one would hear. She wanted to get back to the diary, to read more about Great-Aunt Phoebe without being disturbed.

She almost made it back to her room before a sound behind her startled her, and she whirled around.

"Mrroww."

Scooter padded over and began to rub his face against her

flannel pajama legs, purring loudly enough to wake the dead, and howling intermittently.

"I know you're hungry," Phoebe whispered. "But I can't go down to the kitchen right now."

He continued his protest, and she knew him well enough to realize that he wouldn't stop until he got what he wanted. "This is why you weigh twenty pounds, you know," she hissed at him. At last she surrendered. With Scooter at her heels, she slipped down the stairs and into the kitchen. Scooter headed straight for the pantry, where his food was kept. Phoebe served up a small bowl of kibbles and set it on the floor, watching as he made a beeline for the dish and began to chow down.

Then Phoebe realized that she, too, was hungry. She surveyed the contents of the pantry for something that didn't have to be cooked and came up with a choice between bran cereal or the rest of the oatmeal cookies. "No contest," she muttered, grabbing the cookie bag and retrieving a diet cola out of the fridge. Not exactly a healthy breakfast, but even Scooter's kibbles looked more appetizing than the bran buds. She might even be able to make a case for the merits of oatmeal, if she pushed rationalization to the limit.

Fortunately, her raid on the kitchen hadn't awakened anyone. She made it back to the bedroom a second time without being accosted and was settled in the bed with the diary, the cookies, and the can of pop before she heard the floorboards creak under Hargraves's heavy step.

A light knock sounded on the door, and the nurse's voice whispered, "Phoebe? Are you up?"

Phoebe held her breath and kept silent. After a moment or two, the footsteps receded down the hallway toward Gram's room. Good. The small deception had bought her at least an hour of solitude, time enough to read more in her great-aunt's journal.

She bit into a cookie, brushed the crumbs off the comforter, and picked up the book. Where had she left off last night? January 2, a long entry about Great-Aunt Phoebe's determination to face her problems head-on. She found the place, skimmed back through the discussion about Father, and continued:

Jonathan. Strictly speaking, I can hardly call Jonathan a problem. He is a wonderful man, very caring and considerate. Under other circumstances I could easily imagine myself becoming his wife. Did I really say that? A wife? Is it possible that I am in love with him?

I've been told that when you're in love, you have no doubt about it, but I suspect life is a little more complex than that. I care about Jonathan, and when I am with him, I feel a sense of peace that rarely comes to me at other times. Perhaps I do love him—or am beginning to move in the direction of love. But the situation is complicated by my responsibilities where Lewis is concerned, and I can hardly believe a young man just starting out in life would *be willing to take on both a wife and a six- or seven-year-old child.*

Besides, Jonathan does not really know me. He perceives me as an eighteen-year-old high school senior with a covey of girlfriends and a lighthearted, happy-go-lucky view of the world. He has no idea of what really goes on at home, or what Father is like, or how confused I am about my own future.

How could I possibly explain it to him in a way that he would understand? Even if I did tell him, how could I be sure he would not turn away? Or that if he did ask me to marry him it would not be out of some distorted sense of duty or chivalry? Girls are taught from the cradle that the highest ideal for a woman is to have a handsome knight on a white horse ride in and rescue us from distress. I wonder if that is really the soundest basis upon which to build a lifelong relationship. I am not certain I would want to live forever with someone who sees me as a weak, helpless woman who needs saving.

Phoebe felt something turn over in her stomach as she read the words. How well she identified with Great-Aunt Phoebe! She had never been sure whether or not Jake loved her for herself because she had held back and not let him know what was really inside.

Just like herself, Phoebe's great-aunt felt isolated, caught in a life she could not control and had not wanted. There were bright spots, certainly—especially the close relationship with her little brother, Lewis—but for the most part, what Phoebe had read so far in the diary painted a less-than-hopeful picture. What about all those friends who had written in the Memory Book about their love and admiration for Miss Phoebe Lange? The people who smiled back from the photos with such happiness and contentment?

She shook her head and read on:

Even my best friends, Ethyle and Mildred, do not know the whole story. They love me, I know, and they are constant and faithful friends. Yet I am uncertain of their response, too, were I to tell them about how Father drinks himself into a stupor and ignores me, or into a rage that results in a beating for poor Lewis. Everyone seems to have a mental picture of me that does not correspond with my own. They see me as good and noble and true, courageously facing the loss of my mother and gladly taking on the care of my little brother. They view our family as bravely going forward with life in the face of unspeakable tragedy. And yet the tragedy remains. There has been no healing, just a scabbing over of wounds and a festering of anger and pain below, in the darkness. They do not see my tears, my rage, my aloneness. Only the face I put on—in Mr. Eliot's words, "preparing a face to meet the faces that I meet." The face that protects me from the possibility of further pain.

But the mask is heavy and cumbersome.

Phoebe stopped. From her literature studies, she immediately recognized the allusion to T. S. Eliot's "The Love Song of J. Alfred Prufrock"—had, in fact, once written a final paper in Twentieth-Century Poetry on Eliot's metaphors of superficiality in the poem. Now other images from the poem came back to her: the tea-party conversation, in which the women talk of Michelangelo but never reveal themselves to one another; the figures of death and drowning; and simmering beneath the surface, the unasked, unanswered, terrifying question: "Do I dare disturb the Universe?"

The poem, if Phoebe recalled correctly, had been published only a few years before Great-Aunt Phoebe's diary had been written—around 1920, she thought, give or take a year. And yet it apparently had a profound impact upon Great-Aunt Phoebe, sufficient to stay with her and come out in her personal reflections.

A face to meet the faces that I meet—an apt description, Phoebe thought, of the fear that kept people from being honest with one another. And her great-aunt was right. The mask was heavy and cumbersome. Claustrophobic, even. Peering out from behind a facade. Protecting oneself at the cost of genuine love and acceptance.

A high price to pay. But what other choice did she have?

Phoebe had no answer. And neither, apparently, did her great-aunt.

And so I find myself trapped. Caught in a place where I am surrounded by friends and yet feel totally alone. Even God seems distant and aloof.

The thought of God brings me to the final problem about which I must be ruthlessly honest.

God. All my life I have sought to be a good Christian. I have attended church regularly and prayed faithfully. The Bible has long been a source of comfort and strength for me, and a challenge to become more than I am. "From a child I have known the holy scriptures, which are able to make me wise unto salvation."

In the past few years, however, the Scriptures have gone silent. Prayer seems a futile effort, and God is far away. I wonder if perhaps I have outgrown my childlike faith and am now simply going through the motions, keeping up the facade with God as well as with those around me.

In theory, I believe that God knows me, heart and soul and mind. And yet where I once felt Christ as close to me as my own breath, I now feel only emptiness and silence. If God knows the agony in my heart and cares about it, why does there not come some word of assurance? Perhaps God knows me too well, has seen the pain and anger and frustration that darken my soul, and has turned from me.

I am no theologian, and perhaps these questions are far too deep for my comprehension. I only know that the simple faith that once sustained me has now deserted me, and I am bereft. If even God can discern the truth about me and abandon me, what hope do I have for finding a human hand that will hold to mine, a human heart that will not turn away?

The black ink on the pages of the diary wavered like a landscape through a pouring rain. Phoebe fought to blink back tears. Maybe it had been a mistake, searching out Great-Aunt Phoebe's diary. Such raw anguish and confusion only served to torment her own exposed emotions.

And if just the reading of it was this agonizing, how much worse would it get when Phoebe began to think "honestly and ruthlessly" about her own situation?

Yet she knew she could not simply shut the book and walk

away. She had to see this through to the end, however much pain it cost her.

Pandora's box had been opened. She could only trust that when all the woes of the world had been exhumed, something akin to hope might still remain.

10

Connections

Phoebe didn't tell Gram she had found Great-Aunt Phoebe's diary.

When Hargraves had returned at eight o'clock, this time knocking more forcefully on the door of the tower bedroom and announcing breakfast, Phoebe had stashed the book between the mattress and box springs and jumped up like a guilty teenager caught smoking behind the woodshed. A silly reaction, she knew. And yet she couldn't help feeling that—at least for the time being—she ought to keep the journal a secret, just between herself and her ancestor.

Gram looked better this morning, her voice stronger, her breathing less ragged, a bit more color in her cheeks. "I'll be up and around in no time," she said. "Just having you home is a tonic." She set aside the breakfast tray and fixed Phoebe with an inscrutable gaze. "And how are you doing?"

The remainder of the question hung unasked between them: *How are you doing with this new truth, being the daughter of a murderer?*

Phoebe cut her eyes to the wallpaper over Gram's head and began counting the little pink flowers. "I'm doing fine."

"You've talked with Jake, I assume? Hargraves told me about the roses."

"Sure. He phones. We talk." *But not about this,* Phoebe's mind added. *Never about this.*

"Most men wouldn't be that thoughtful," Gram said. "He's a keeper, your Jake."

A keeper. Phoebe let her mind circle around the image. Like a large-mouthed bass. The best catch of the season. A trophy to be stuffed and hung on the wall. Or fileted and breaded for the big fish fry. Jake was a catch, all right. The prize she had won for being dishonest, for hiding the truth and guarding her soul.

A cool, light hand touched her fingers. "You seem distracted, dear," Gram was saying. "Are you feeling all right?"

Phoebe hedged. "Actually, I'm a little tired. I didn't sleep very well, and I woke up with a headache."

Gram smiled and patted her arm. "Hargraves told me about all the cleaning you did yesterday. I appreciate it, I really do. But perhaps you should take it easy today. Get some rest."

"I'll do that." Phoebe latched onto the chance to get away. What she needed most was to be alone—alone with Great-Aunt

Phoebe's diary. "Maybe I'll just go to my room and read for a while."

"That sounds like a good idea. You go on. Don't bother with the tray—Hargraves will pick it up."

"All right, Gram. I'll see you later." Phoebe kissed her grandmother on the cheek and made her exit. Once outside in the hallway, with the door shut behind her, she exhaled a sigh of relief and bolted for the tower.

—

January 8, 1927

I spent the day with Ethyle and Mildred, doing a little shopping and having lunch at a small café on the square. What was originally intended to be an afternoon of fun turned out to be more of an inquisition—with me as the object of interrogation.

The first line of questioning had to do with my relationship with Jonathan. Was I in love with him? Had he kissed me yet? Were we talking about marriage?

I spoiled their game, I fear, by playing coy and not telling them a bit of what they wanted to hear. Whether or not I have kissed Jonathan is no one's business but my own. (Yes, I have, and it was quite the most wonderful kiss I could ever imagine—everything short of harpsichord music and fireworks. I doubt even Rudolph Valentino could hold a candle to Jonathan Barksdale in that department.) Still, my love life is not a matter for gossip or speculation, even among my closest friends. Moreover, I am a very long way from admitting to being in love with him or any man, much less discussing marriage.

Once the subject of Jonathan was exhausted, the two of them became most uncomfortably solicitous. They were worried about me, Ethyle said, because I seemed so withdrawn and distant. Mildred agreed, adding that if there was some kind of trouble brewing at home, I should understand that I could confide in them. Perhaps Lewis was doing poorly in school, or Father was having financial difficulties, they hinted.

I could not help feeling as if the shopping trip and luncheon were simply a diversion to shroud a fishing expedition. They mean well, and I have no doubt that they genuinely care about me, but if they were to know the real reasons behind my detachment, they might not be so eager to stay at my side and stand with me against the threat that Father poses both to me and to Lewis.

The danger to Lewis is much more immediate than any hazard to my own person. Father strapped him again last night, and (coward that I am) I dared not interfere. Some bigger boys at school had been bullying Lewis and rather than fight them, he simply ran away. I was very proud of him for his courage, but when Father heard Lewis crying and learned the cause, he flew into a rage and said that no son of his would grow up to be a sniveling pantywaist.

I stood outside the door to Father's study, listening as the strap fell until I could stand it no longer, then I went to my room and wept. I prayed, too, begging God to intervene where I could not, but no help came. All I could do was wait and tend my precious brother's wounds after the beating was over.

I stayed in the tower until I heard Lewis's bedroom door shut and I was certain Father had gone back into his study. Then, armed with cleansing cloths and anti-septic, I entered Lewis's room to find him lying across the bed. For the first time, Father had drawn blood, and Lewis's thin little legs were covered with welts. I doctored them the best I could and tried to ease his suffering with comforting words, but he did not respond. He just lay there, neither crying nor flinching when the painful antiseptic touched the raw flesh. His little face was set like stone, and when I had finished and tried to gather him into my arms, he stiffened and would not yield to the embrace. "I'll show him," he muttered. "I'll show him I can be a man. I'll never cry again. Never."

I feel so weak, so helpless. I cannot help wondering what Mother would have done. Would she have been strong enough to stand up to a rage like Father's? Or would she have given in, as I did, and simply tried to mop up the mess after it was over?

Perhaps Lewis can steel himself not to cry, but I cannot. Afterwards, I went to my bedroom, locked the door, and wept for an hour, until all my tears were spent. Then I prayed, or tried to, but the only word that would come was, "Why?"

Why is God absent when we need help most?

Why do my pleas go unanswered?

Why is heaven silent?

"Suffer the little children," Jesus said. But the children are suffering, and no one seems to care.

Yes, my friends are right. I have withdrawn from them. How can I do otherwise? I am ashamed. Ashamed of my father, and ashamed of myself. I am angry— with life, with my own weakness, even with God.

And so I am caught. I cannot confess my anger and shame to Ethyle and Mildred, or even to Jonathan. They've never listened to their own brother being beaten and done nothing about it. I cannot confess to God, for God already knows and has remained silent.

Long ago I lost my mother. I have lost my father to drink and rage. I am losing my brother one bit at a time. Perhaps I have even lost God.

I am alone.

Alone, and afraid.

Phoebe swiped away tears and lay back against the pillow. Something inside her wanted to scream at Great-Aunt Phoebe: *Tell someone! Get help! You don't have to be alone!*

But of course, she couldn't. Great-Aunt Phoebe was long gone. She couldn't hear her namesake imploring her to reach out, to connect, to find aid and solace and strength among those who loved her. It was all done, finished. Nothing Phoebe might say or do now would alter what had already happened. Great-Aunt Phoebe would die in a car accident. Little Lewis would be left without an advocate, would continue to be dominated and intimidated by his father, and would in turn do the same to his own son. The sins of the fathers, visited upon the children for generations.

Phoebe empathized with her great-aunt. She understood too well those feelings of aloneness, of utter isolation. And for all her inner urgings, she also comprehended why Great-Aunt Phoebe could not tell a soul what was really happening in the Lange household. How she wept at night because she could not protect her brother, how she raged at God for standing by while people suffered.

Phoebe knew all about anger and fear and shame, knew how it felt to be trapped.

Still, it was sad.

And there was nothing anyone could do.

～

The telephone rang—once, then a second time. Phoebe could hear Hargraves's heavy step on the floor below, crossing the front parlor.

119

"Phoebe?" The nurse's voice drifted up the stairs, sounding oddly muffled through the closed door to the tower room. "Phoebe? Telephone for you!"

Phoebe jerked upright and stuffed the diary into its hiding place between the mattress and box springs. There it was—that childish twinge of guilt again, as if she had just escaped being caught doing something naughty. She shook it off, shoved her feet into her slippers, and padded down the stairs.

Hargraves handed her the receiver and stalked away.

"Hello?"

"Phoebe, it's Jake."

"And Krista!" a second voice added.

"And Naomi!" A feminine chuckle came through the receiver.

Phoebe felt a surge of joy rise up in her. "All three of you? Together? Where are you?"

There was laughter on the other end of the line and a few jumbled words as both Krista and Naomi tried to talk at the same time.

"We're on the extension in the bedroom," Krista said. "Jake is in the living room."

"At my apartment," Jake said. "They . . . ah, they came over, and we decided to call you."

Something in his voice didn't sound quite right. As if he were hiding something, not quite telling the whole truth.

"We miss you," Krista said. "Are you doing all right?"

"Yes, I'm fine."

Naomi's voice came on the line again. "How's your grandmother?"

"Better. Not well yet, but better."

"We, uh . . . well, we miss you," Krista said.

"You said that already, Krista." Phoebe leaned against the wall in the hall and tucked the receiver between her shoulder and her ear. "I miss all of you, too. But you sound like you're up to something. What's going on?"

She heard a rustle and some whispers, and then Naomi's *sotto* voice: "Let Jake do it."

"Let Jake do wha—"

"How would you feel about a little company this weekend?" Jake broke in.

"Company? What do you mean?"

"We thought we'd drive up to Asheville and see you," Krista said. "You wouldn't have to put us up, with your grandmother ill and all. We could get a couple rooms. We just want to see you, that's all. Take you out to dinner. Talk with you face to face."

Phoebe pushed off the wall and shifted the receiver to the other ear. "Talk to me about what? It sounds like you've got an agenda, and I think I should know what it is."

Jake sighed into the phone. "All right. We've been discussing things, Phoebe, and we're all convinced that something's wrong. You've been distant, preoccupied."

"Of course I'm preoccupied. Gram has pneumonia."

"It's more than that," Jake insisted. "Whatever it is, we want to help. We want to be there for you, to support you."

"Right," Krista interrupted. "We love you, Phoebe. We're your best friends."

"I know." Phoebe stifled an exasperated sigh. "And I love you, too—all of you. This is just not a good time for you to come."

"Then talk to us now," Jake said. "You can tell us what's bothering you."

Phoebe thought about the newspaper article—about her father's crime, her mother's death. A few minutes ago, she had wanted to shout at Great-Aunt Phoebe, *Tell someone!* Now she steeled herself for the lie: "Nothing's wrong. Honest. I'm just a little stressed out right now with Gram's illness. But I'm handling it pretty well. Everything will be all right." There was a long silence, a space of dead air. "Jake? Krista? Naomi? Are you still there?"

"We're here." It was Naomi, quiet, subdued.

"We'll always be here," Krista added.

"Thanks." Phoebe closed her eyes and sagged against the wall.

"I guess we'll hang up now," Jake said. "Keep in touch, Phoebe. Please. We love you, and we'll be praying for you."

Praying. Phoebe bit her lip, and a sarcastic reply formed in her mind: *As if that would change anything.* Instead she said, "Thanks for calling, guys. I appreciate it."

Naomi and Krista said their good-byes and hung up the extension. Only Jake was left. She could hear him breathing. "Phoebe?"

"Yes?"

"Take care of yourself."

"I will, Jake. You, too. Bye now."

As the line clicked and went dead, she heard an echo in her mind, Krista's parting words: *"We'll always be here."*

Phoebe held the phone against her chest and exhaled a long breath.

"Always," she'd said.

But the world was so uncertain and security so fragile. How could anyone promise forever?

Phoebe had been sitting on the second step for nearly half an hour when Hargraves came back through the front parlor and started upstairs. "I'm doing laundry," the nurse said curtly. "You got any clothes you want washed, tell me now. I'm going up to get your sheets." She stepped around Phoebe and began clomping up the stairs.

With a jolt, Phoebe came to her senses. If Hargraves stripped her bed, she would find the diary. Phoebe jumped up and ran after her. "Wait!"

Hargraves turned. "What?"

"You don't have to do that—change my bed, I mean. I've only been here a few nights. Just give me a minute to get my stuff together. Then I'll come help with the laundry."

The nurse surveyed her with a critical eye. "All right." She turned on her heel and descended into the lower regions of the house.

Phoebe ran for the tower room and shut the door behind her. She gathered up a few dirty clothes and piled them in one corner, then retrieved the diary and sank down on the unmade bed. Why it was so important that no one else know about Great-Aunt Phoebe's journal she could not articulate. All she had to go on was a gut feeling that the words written in it were for her eyes only—hers, and Great-Aunt Phoebe's, of course.

Maybe it had to do with connections. The sense of identification Phoebe felt with her great-aunt and with the life she had led. The similarities between them. A bond that reached across the decades, even from death to life.

That was it. A bond. A sacred trust. And Phoebe would guard it, no matter what.

She made the bed hurriedly, then dragged the platform rocker over to the side of the wardrobe and stepped up onto the seat.

She would replace the journal in its original hiding place on top of the wardrobe. No one would think to look for it there. After all, it had been safe from prying eyes for the past seventy-five years. Even Grandpa Lewis hadn't been able to find it.

Taking the journal in one hand, Phoebe braced the other against the side of the wardrobe and reached toward the top. Just a little higher, a little farther . . .

She stretched. The diary dropped out of her hand onto the top of the wardrobe, but once it was safe in its place, Phoebe couldn't reverse her momentum. The rocking chair shifted. The room lurched.

And then, as in her dream, Phoebe felt herself falling. But there were no stars. Only the blur of the tower room around her. A sickening jolt as her head struck something hard.

And everything went dark.

PART 2

Remnants of the Past

*Today is but a fragment
of forever.
Threads of time tangle
around my heart,
twine through my mind,
and tie me to my history.
Even what I cannot see
becomes a part of me,
and shadows of the past
inform my knowing,
drawing me toward oneness
with myself.*

11

We Are One

Phoebe opened her eyes and found herself lying on her bed in the tower room. Everything looked foggy, distorted, as if she viewed her surroundings from under water. Her bedside alarm clock was nowhere to be found, but from the slant of the light she could tell it was late afternoon.

Had she slept straight through the day and into the evening?

She tried to get up, but her head throbbed mercilessly, and she sank back onto the pillow. Through the open window, noises seemed magnified a thousand times. The rattling slam of a car door. The blaring of a horn—one of those annoying ones teenagers put on hot rods to make that loud "ah-oog-ah" sound. The honking continued. She pulled the pillow over her head and tried to block it out.

Then, from downstairs, a gruff voice: "Phoebe! Get down here! Your young man is here!"

It didn't sound like Hargraves, but then everything seemed

muddled by the pounding in her brain. Phoebe pulled the pillow off her face, opened her eyes, and blinked. Jake? Here? Impossible!

"I'm coming!" she yelled, even though the noise of her own voice only exacerbated the headache.

She rose to a sitting position and slid to the edge of the bed. Something wasn't right. Her legs, for one thing. She was wearing stockings—white stockings. And a long-waisted navy dress with a sailor's tie. On the floor next to the bed were a pair of black shoes with huge silver buckles, like something she'd wear to portray a pilgrim in a Thanksgiving pageant.

Phoebe got up and went to the mirror. The reflection that stared back at her seemed younger, but it might have been just a play of the light. Dark eyes. Brown hair with a tint of auburn, brushed back in short waves from her face.

Her haircut looked different. And what was up with this dress?

An eerie sense of disconnection washed over her, and she gazed around. The room was the same, and not the same. New curtains—still those long panels in off-white lace, but a different design. An antique lamp on the bedside table. Lace doilies on the dresser, and a drop-front writing desk under the west window. And on the desk, a couple of books lay open, surrounded by a litter of clippings and photographs and a dark-brown jar of glue.

The Memory Book. And Great-Aunt Phoebe's diary.

Phoebe went to the desk. The Memory Book, its cover stiff and dark and new, lay pushed to one side, with some loose photos sticking out at odd angles. The diary, centered on the desk as if someone had been writing in it, was open about two-thirds of the way through the book. The page was blank, except for a date written at the top:

Friday, May 6, 1927

A week before graduation. Seven days before Great-Aunt Phoebe's death.

Phoebe was just about to page backwards through the diary when the door to the tower room burst open. Phoebe snapped the book shut and turned. A small boy stood in the doorway, leaning on the doorjamb and trying to catch his breath. He wore tweed knickers and a white collarless shirt and had a Buster Brown haircut that needed trimming.

Phoebe stared at him for a moment. It couldn't be. But it was. The child in the photo, leaning on Great-Aunt Phoebe. Her grandfather. Lewis Lange. Six years old.

"Lewis?" her voice shook.

"I hope your headache's better, Sis, because you gotta come downstairs NOW. He's here, and Papa's got him in the parlor giving him the third degree. And—" He grinned broadly. "He's got a brand-new Model T Roadster—dark blue, with a canvas top and a rumble seat. It's a pip, Sis, a real pip. He said he'd take us both for a drive. Come on—he's waiting!"

Phoebe's mind spun. This was a dream. It had to be. And yet

it seemed so . . . real. She frowned at him. "Who are you talking about?"

"Jonathan, of course. He's downstairs waiting right now." The boy gazed at her with a curious expression. "What's eatin' you, Phoeb?" He pointed to the book she held in her hands. "Oh, I get it. You're writing in your precious diary. Writing about Jonathan, I bet." He took on a childish singsong tone. "About how *handsome* he is, and how much he *loves* you, and how you want him to *hug* you and *kiss* you, and—" He lunged toward her and made a grab for the diary, but Phoebe was too fast for him. She held it above his head, out of his reach even when he jumped as high as he could. "Come on, Sis, let me have a look. I read real good, y'know."

"Absolutely not." Phoebe shook her head. "Go on downstairs and tell Jonathan I'm coming." She swatted him on the backside with the diary and shooed him from the room.

When he was gone, she sank onto the bed and let out a breath. If this were a dream, it was the most distinct, authentic dream she had ever had. She pinched the inside of her arm, hard, but although she felt the pain, it made no difference. She was still here, apparently in 1927, having taken Great-Aunt Phoebe's place like Sam Beckett in the old television series *Quantum Leap*.

Well, she had wanted answers. She had wanted to know about Great-Aunt Phoebe's life, had been convinced that somehow the past held the key to her future. But unlike Dr. Beckett, Phoebe had no computer-generated hologram to guide her, and she hadn't the faintest idea what to do next.

She looked down. The diary lay in her lap. She opened the front cover and saw her name—or rather, Great-Aunt Phoebe's name—on the inside face page. She turned to the first entry.

January 1, 1927
The New Year has come, and all day everyone has been talking about last night's party and formulating New Year's resolutions. And yet, with the turning of this page, I find myself with far more questions than resolutions.

An impatient voice called up the stairs, a voice Phoebe didn't recognize. Father. It had to be Father.

"Phoebe! Get down here—now!" he shouted.

The diary would have to wait. For a while, anyway.

All during the ride around town in the rattling tin lizzie, Phoebe listened to Lewis's nonstop chatter from the rumble seat and she watched Jonathan's interaction with the boy. Patient and affable, he endured Lewis's insistent questions about the new car with grace and good humor, showed him how to shift the gears, gave him a history lesson about Mr. Henry Ford and the innovation of a mass-production assembly line for his Model T.

It didn't take long for Phoebe to understand why her great-aunt had been drawn to Jonathan Barksdale. He was handsome, with sandy hair, a wispy blond mustache, and bright blue eyes. And obviously well-to-do, if he could afford such an automobile. But his attractiveness went far deeper than a dazzling smile and a new blue Roadster. There was something else about him—something solid and deep. A kindness of heart, a nobility of spirit. An ineffable goodness that came out in the way he treated both her and Lewis.

She could hardly believe she was thinking this way. All her life she had kept herself distant from others, especially men. Something within her—something she couldn't identify—waved red flags, warning her of danger. Maybe subconsciously, Phoebe had known all along what had really happened the night her mother died. Perhaps the truth had been buried within her for twenty years, coming out only in a nameless reluctance to trust.

And yet she liked Jonathan Barksdale. She felt at ease with him, in a way she had never felt comfortable with any man.

But of course, it was only a dream, she reminded herself.

The Model T was, as Lewis had declared, "a real pip," a shiny blue two-seater with leather upholstery and a convertible canvas top. They drove down Charlotte Street and crawled up Macon Avenue to the ritzy Grove Park Inn, where they sipped lemonade and watched the sunset from the terrace.

Below them, to the west, the mountain vistas of the Blue Ridge spread out in the distance like layers of folded velvet, purple and gray and green. Lewis amused himself by exploring the huge great room. "The fireplace is so big you could drive the

Roadster right into it!" he announced on one of his passes through the open terrace. When he was gone again, Jonathan turned to Phoebe and fixed his gaze on her.

"Is he doing all right?"

"Who? Lewis?" Phoebe hesitated. "I suppose so."

Jonathan leaned forward and took her hand. "You can be honest with me, Phoebe."

The touch startled her, and she pulled away slightly. "I don't know what you mean."

"Yes, you do. You can trust me, Phoebe. You should realize that by now. I love you. And I care about Lewis, too." He stared into her eyes, forcing her to meet his gaze. "I'm concerned about the boy. And about you."

Phoebe felt tears prick her eyes. Lewis was a sweet child, an energetic, affectionate little boy. Still impressionable. Still able to change, to avoid becoming the kind of man he eventually turned out to be. And Jonathan was offering his help, his support.

Just as Jake had on the telephone.

A powerful sense of déjà vu washed over her. But Jonathan wasn't real. He was a dream, a projection of her subconscious mind, a figment of her imagination. He had to be.

And if he were only a dream, maybe she should just play along, take on Great-Aunt Phoebe's role the way Sam Beckett did in the TV show. Maybe she ought to confide in him, tell him what was going on with her father and with Lewis. He might be able to see the situation more clearly and know what to do. Perhaps if she let him in, just a little, he could—

What was she thinking? This wasn't real, and it wasn't an episode of *Quantum Leap*. She couldn't change the past, couldn't set right what once had gone wrong. She couldn't do anything, except watch and listen and learn.

And apparently she wasn't doing a very good job of listening. Jonathan was halfway through a sentence, and she didn't have a clue what he was talking about.

"So he could come and live with us," he was saying.

Phoebe held up a hand. "Wait. Repeat that, please?"

"I said, we could get married. Next weekend, right after graduation. I've got a good job, and enough money put aside. We can take a few days' honeymoon—here, if you like." He waved his hand to indicate the opulent Grove Park Inn. "And then we can rent a little house. Lewis can come to live with us."

"Get married?" Phoebe felt her jaw drop.

"Sure. Why not?" He winked at her. "I'm your Sheik, and you're my Sheba, remember?"

"Yes, but—"

"Some of our friends have already tied the knot." He leaned forward and captured her hand. "Look, Phoebe, it just makes sense. I don't know what's going on with you and Lewis, but I can see in your eyes that things aren't right. And I can see it in Lewis, too. Right now, this afternoon, away from home, he's a perfectly happy little boy. Relaxed and carefree, as a child should be. But he's not always like this, is he? There's a darkness about him, a shadow that comes over him. Something simmering under the surface." His face took on a serious, determined expression. "I can help, Phoebe. Let me help."

"Jake—" Phoebe caught herself, but not in time. "Jonathan, I mean. I'm not sure I'm ready to get married."

He narrowed his eyes. "Who's Jake? Phoebe, is there somebody else?"

"No, of course not."

"Then what? I do love you, you know. We could have a wonderful future together. A future that includes your little brother. I'm not asking you to give him up. I'm only asking to be allowed to be part of your lives."

Her mind reeled. She groped for words. But she was spared in her search by Lewis, who dashed back onto the terrace and grabbed her hand. "Look, Sis!" He pointed toward the horizon, where the sun had gone behind a cloud and was sending out bands of light toward the top of the mountains. "It's like God smiling down from heaven."

Phoebe turned her eyes to Jonathan. He was still staring intently at her, waiting for an answer. "We'll discuss this later."

"All right. Later." He sighed and turned his eyes toward the horizon. "But know this: I won't give up. I'll keep on knocking, until you open the door and let me in."

The simple words triggered a memory within Phoebe—a visual image of the classic painting that hung in the fellowship hall of the church she had attended years before. Jesus knocking at the door of the heart. She heard the familiar words from Sunday school: "Ask, and it will be given you; seek, and you shall find; knock, and the door shall be opened."

She gazed off into the sunset and thought of Lewis seeing God's smile in the clouds. *I wish you would look down on me and tell me what to do,* Phoebe thought miserably.

When no answer came, she forced a smile of her own and squeezed Jonathan's hand.

12

Phoebe's Truth

S mile, everyone! Lewis, get closer to your sister."

Jonathan peered out from behind the camera, and Lewis, standing on the front porch next to Phoebe, leaned in toward her. She looked down at him, then reached to smooth his wind-ruffled hair. He grinned up at her—a boyish, trusting expression.

When, Phoebe wondered, did it become so difficult to trust? Was vulnerability one of the lost arts of childhood, something you grew out of when you got too big to sit in your mother's lap? Did it happen brick by brick, a wall going up unnoticed; or all at once, a door slamming shut?

She gazed out into the yard, where she could just see the top of Jonathan's sandy head over the boxy camera. This wonderful man wanted to marry her—well, not her, exactly—and yet she found herself hesitating, pulling back, just as she retreated every time Jake got too close.

The late-afternoon sun slanted through the trees, casting a bronze glow over the porch and touching Lewis's Buster Brown hair with golden highlights.

"We're losing the light," Jonathan called. "This is the last one. Now, smile!"

Phoebe put her arm around Lewis's shoulders, and he snuggled up next to her.

"Got it—perfect!" Jonathan came out from behind his camera and punched Lewis playfully on the arm. "That will be a great one for my photography club project at the Farm School."

Phoebe racked her brain. Hadn't Warren Wilson College been called the Farm School in the twenties? So Jonathan was a college man.

All afternoon she had been piecing together information about Jonathan Barksdale. His father, Eugene, operated the Majestic Theater at the corner of Market and College Streets. Jonathan worked with him as weekend manager. It was, as Jonathan had said, a good job, and eventually he could take over the entire operation of the place himself—maybe even buy it. But apparently Jonathan wanted more than a job—he wanted a degree and a career that, in his words, would "take him somewhere."

Where would his life take him if, at age twenty, he married a girl straight out of high school and took on the responsibility of supporting not only her but her little brother as well?

It was an insane idea. Motivated by a good heart, no doubt, but insane nevertheless.

Jonathan put his camera into a box strapped on the running board of the Model T Roadster and came back to the porch. "Phoebe, you might want to get a shawl," he said. "Now that the sun's going down, it's getting chilly."

Phoebe stared at him. "Are we going somewhere?"

"It's Saturday. You promised to have dinner with me, remember? And then the premiere of *Ben-Hur*?" He shook his head and laughed. "I know you've seemed preoccupied all afternoon, but I can't believe you'd forget. You've talked of nothing else for a week."

"Oh. Of course. I'll just be a minute." She left Jonathan standing on the porch steps and went to enter the house, only to find Lewis blocking her path. He looked up at her, and although he said not a word, his face spoke volumes. She knelt down and put her arms around him. He held on so tight her ribs ached. She thought her heart might break.

"I'm sorry, sweetie," she whispered into his hair. "You can't go this time, but you'll be all right, won't you? I'll fix you something to eat before I leave. And I'll be home as soon as I can."

He bit his lip and nodded bravely. "I can take care of myself. I'll read the new book you bought me. And I'll stay out of Father's way."

Phoebe felt her insides constrict. She wanted to pick him up and take him with her, never to let him out of her sight again. But she didn't. Instead, she steeled herself to go inside, retrieve a wrap, and make him a plate of whatever she could find in the kitchen.

~

From Phoebe's perspective, the "World's Greatest Show" turned out to be a bust. She had never liked subtitled films—it was far too distracting to try to watch the actors and read the words simultaneously. A silent movie was even worse. She tried to pay attention, but she kept finding herself comparing the grainy, jerky movements on the black-and-white screen to the sweeping Technicolor images of the Charlton Heston version of *Ben-Hur*. Even as she sat in the flickering light of the balcony with Jonathan's arm around her shoulder, her mind translated the scenes in front of her to the modern remake.

The biblical themes and images of the miraculous in the film bothered her more than she wanted to admit. Her mind kept wandering, and disturbing thoughts nagged at her. In the movie, God intervened in the world in such tangible ways. The crucifixion of Christ, a central motif in the film, brought healing and hope and changed lives.

Twentieth-century Christians seemed to have such a sterilized, spiritualized view of the event: the noble sacrifice of God's only Son, the eternal Savior sent to earth in human form, his primary mission to die for the sins of the world. This was the generally accepted view of what Jesus' death meant to humankind. And yet Phoebe couldn't shake the anger that rose up in her when she viewed the crucifixion on the screen of her mind. For the first time, she came to the familiar scene with the perspective of knowing what it meant for a father to abuse his only son. Every lash that fell across Jesus' back echoed the crack of Father's belt on little Lewis's tender legs. The whole idea sent a shiver of rage through her soul. How could any father, even a Divine Father, stand by and watch such torture?

Everyone around her seemed to accept the premise that "God is love," and yet much of what was attributed to God didn't seem at all loving. And not just the crucifixion, either. Whole nations of people in the Old Testament wiped out—every living thing killed, including women and the elderly, toddlers, even babes in arms. Could such slaughter truly be God's will? Was all this bloodshed necessary to bring souls into relationship with the Almighty?

And—the most important question of all, in Phoebe's estimation—could little Lewis's abuse, and the pattern that resulted in her mother's death, possibly be the will of God? Part of some kind of inscrutable cosmic plan?

It was all so confusing, and frightening as well. Phoebe could hardly believe she was thinking like this. Did raising such questions make her a hopeless heretic? Or was God, the God she had always tried to believe in, big enough to embrace her doubts as well as her faith?

~

When Phoebe arrived home, the house was dark and quiet. She kissed Jonathan good night on the front porch, then went inside and tiptoed upstairs with her shoes in her hand.

Lewis's door was open a crack, and she went inside. Amid a tangle of linens she could see his thin little chest rising and falling in the shallow breathing of dreamless slumber. She straightened the covers and tucked the blanket around his shoulders. A wave of tenderness rose up in her, a mother's love for the child who, technically, was her own grandfather. She reached to brush her fingers over his hair, and he stirred and opened his eyes.

"Phoebe?" he mumbled, his voice slurred with sleep.

"It's me, Lewis," she whispered. "I just came to check on you and say good night."

"I read the book, and I really liked it. But it would have been more fun if you had been here."

"We'll read it together soon."

He turned over and smiled drowsily at her. "I'm going back to sleep now."

"That's good. I'll see you tomorrow." She turned to leave, but something inside wouldn't let her go. A powerful longing rose up from some deep place in her soul, insistent upon expression.

She returned to his side, leaned down, and kissed him on the forehead. "I love you, Lewis."

It was so easy, so natural. So true.

She had said the words before—to Gram, to Jake, even to Krista and Naomi. And she *did* love her grandmother, her fiancé, and her friends, as much as she was capable of understanding love. Yet her love for them had cost her little. She had not been vulnerable, had not laid herself open before them. She had risked nothing in loving them. She had kept herself protected.

Now, for the first time in her life, Phoebe knew what *I love you* really meant. Love was not warm fuzzy feelings or soft romantic words. It was strength and determination and power. It was a mother bear defending her cubs, a lioness guarding her pride. She knew she would do anything in her power to protect this child, and to love him with all that was within her.

And despite her earlier questions and confusion, she knew something else, too, with a certainty that came upon her so suddenly, so instinctively, that it had to be real.

She knew that God had wept when Jesus suffered and died.

13

A Dream Within a Dream

Phoebe went into the tower bedroom and shut the door. Down the hall, she could hear Father's intermittent snoring. On the other side of the tower, she could imagine Lewis snuggling in under his blanket, sinking into the untroubled sleep of childhood.

But his childhood hadn't been untroubled, had it? And although children were remarkably resilient little beings, Phoebe feared he was approaching that invisible line, that point of no return beyond which even a sensitive, caring boy like Lewis might not be able to recover.

Correction: she *knew* that invisible line existed, *knew* that someday Lewis would cross it, would grow up to be like his father. She just didn't know where the line was, how much the lad could take without being scarred for life. And she didn't know what she could possibly do to change the inevitable.

She turned on the lamp, put on a white cotton nightgown

she found in one of the dresser drawers, and settled into bed with Great-Aunt Phoebe's diary on her lap. Maybe his sister—his *real* sister—could offer some insights into the situation.

Phoebe paused with the book in her hands. How strange this felt, being cast back in time, back to 1927, taking on the role of her great-aunt at age eighteen. She knew her mind had to be playing tricks on her, drawing from her immersion in the Memory Book and her discovery of the diary to create such a vivid dream.

For it had to be a dream. There was no other rational explanation. And yet it felt so . . . so *authentic*. As if she were really here, a stand-in playing Great-Aunt Phoebe's part.

Still, she believed that dreams, especially realistic dreams like this one, were an attempt by the subconscious to communicate truth to the conscious mind. If she could manage to immerse herself fully in the experience, perhaps the necessary enlightenment would come to the surface. Perhaps the dream itself would tell her what to do in her own life.

Exhaling tension on a sigh, Phoebe opened the journal and began to read. She skipped the early entries, the ones she had read before, and skimmed through several weeks' worth of ordinary diary-keeping: a record of Great-Aunt Phoebe's birthday party, some anxieties about midterm exams, the celebration of being named valedictorian. But when she ran across more accounts of the problems Great-Aunt Phoebe had enumerated at the beginning of the journal, Phoebe slowed down and began to read more carefully:

Mildred and Ethyle went after me again today, trying to get me to tell them what has been bothering me. They complain that I am distant and preoccupied, and that even when I am with them, I seem to be somewhere else. And they are right, of course. I am preoccupied. But I cannot bring myself to tell them why.

"Nice" families like ours do not have such concerns. Nice families have fathers who are loving and devoted. Nice families care for each other and protect each other. To paint a different picture, even to my closest friends, would be a betrayal. It would bring shame upon our family name. And it would not change anything. Rather, if Father discovered that I had told anyone how he treats my little brother, or about his drinking, he would no doubt become enraged and take his anger out on Lewis in worse ways than I can imagine.

I can only admit the truth here, where no one can see: I am afraid of my own father. And thus I have no recourse but to keep silent and to try to protect Lewis in the best way I know how.

Phoebe felt a rush of anger rise up in her. *But don't you see, Phoebe, you're not protecting him?* her mind shouted. *Lewis is still getting hurt, and your silence is not helping! You're simply enabling your father's abusiveness by keeping quiet.*

But her great-aunt didn't know anything about enabling,

Phoebe reasoned after the first wave of fury passed. She didn't understand that by remaining silent and keeping the peace, she was merely perpetuating a pattern that would continue to escalate for generations, until it ended in murder.

She calmed herself and continued to read:

> Jonathan, too, is encouraging me to talk, although he does it in gentler, more entreating ways. I fear he may know more than he is telling. I am certain that Lewis would not deliberately reveal what Father does to him; he is much too ashamed to be that forthcoming, even with Jonathan. Lewis adores him and hangs on him at every possible opportunity. Still, Jonathan may have picked up on clues or seen the bruises somehow. And although Father is usually sober (or only getting started) when Jonathan comes to the house, I wonder if Jonathan might not also suspect about Father's excessive drinking.
>
> It makes me so weary to hide all the time, to watch every word and be cautious not to let anything slip. I must constantly be on guard lest I inadvertently say something that would give away the truth.

The more Phoebe read, the more convinced she became that her great-aunt had simply made matters worse by not revealing the truth—to Jonathan, to her friends, to *someone*. She knew all too well what that kind of secret keeping was like, how it drained a person's energy and left one numb and enervated. And yet she understood, too, why Great-Aunt Phoebe felt as if she had no choice in the matter. Telling the truth might only make matters worse. Telling the truth meant risking the loss of everything she loved, everyone she cared for.

I stumble through the days in a red haze, seething with anger and exerting enormous energy to cover it up. I am primarily furious with Father, of course, for drowning himself in drink and taking out his rage on his helpless son. But I am also angry with myself for my weakness, and—if I am truly to be honest—angry with God.

I have spent my whole life believing. When Mother was alive and our home was filled with love and laughter, it was easy to believe in a God who cared, a God who was intimately involved with our lives, the source of all our blessings, and the object of our worship. But now it seems as if Lewis was the final blessing. After his birth, the hand of God was withdrawn from us.

Mother's death I might have understood, and not blamed God. Dreadful things happen in this world. People we love die, and we go on and learn to live again. I was always taught that no matter what happens, God is still with us, and will give us the strength and courage we need to find peace in the midst of pain.

But I can find no peace. I find only isolation and loneliness and the terrifying sense that God has abandoned and betrayed me.

Phoebe shut the book and leaned back against the headboard. Her eyes felt gritty, and she rubbed a hand across them. She was tired. So tired.

Tired of pretending. Tired of covering up. Tired of questions with no answers, and revelations that led not to light but to deeper darkness. Tired of isolation and separation.

She slipped the journal into the drawer of the bedside table, slid under the covers, and turned out the light. Then exhaustion overtook her and she slept.

～

The sun had begun to set behind a grassy hillside in the clearing of a forest. Only the last curve of light remained, a bright orange arc that lengthened the shadows and cast eerie shapes across the land. Phoebe felt herself hovering above the scene, a feather on the wind, watching. Someone was on the hill, lying down with arms outstretched. A child. Observing the clouds, perhaps. Finding shapes in them, the way she and her friends used to do when she was a girl.

She smiled and moved closer to see better. The warmth faded, and ice filled her veins. It wasn't a child. It was a crucifix. A small crucifix, barely four feet long. On it was impaled a diminutive corpus, beardless, its eyes closed and its forehead pierced with thorns. And on the ground next to it, a man, kneeling in worship.

The realism of the crucifix appalled her, and Phoebe tried to turn her eyes away. She had seen figures of the Crucified One before, certainly, in churches and cathedrals she had visited. But her own religious tradition took its symbol from the empty cross, sign of the resurrected Christ. Not this bloody figure of death.

Just as she averted her eyes, her peripheral vision caught a flash of movement. She heard a clanging sound, iron against iron. She turned and looked again.

The man was not worshiping as she had thought. He was driving nails into the corpus's hands and feet. And the figure on the cross wasn't a corpus at all—it was a small boy, his eyes wide with terror, his hair plastered to his head with sweat and blood.

The child made no sound, not even when the spikes pierced his wrists and ankles, anchoring his hands and feet to the wood. He gazed up in Phoebe's direction, his eyes imploring, as if he could see her hovering above him.

The man finished his gruesome task and stood, casting aside the hammer and wiping his palms on the back of his pants. Then he leaned down, lifted up the cross, and dropped it into a hole already dug on the side of the hill.

The child's body shuddered when the base of the cross hit bottom, and he sagged against the iron spikes. His mouth

153

opened, and although Phoebe could not hear him speak, she watched as his lips formed a single, silent word: *Father*. The man stood back to admire his handiwork for a moment, then spat on the ground, and walked away.

The shadows deepened. The last rays of the sun painted the clouds a deep vermilion, as if the sky itself were bleeding. Phoebe desperately wanted to do something to help the child, but she couldn't reach him. All she could do was float above him and watch as his eyes sought hers in that look of resignation.

A shadow moved to the right, at the edge of the forest. Phoebe watched as a young woman with short brown hair crept to the perimeter of the clearing and stood there, weeping. To the left a second figure stirred. Another woman. Then a third. Finally, when the last rays of the sun were almost gone, a fourth figure appeared. A fair-haired man, dressed in a white shirt that stood out like moonlight against the dark branches of the trees.

"Help him!" Phoebe cried, but in the dream her voice came out as barely a whisper.

Whether the man heard her or not, Phoebe could not tell, but he ran forward into the clearing and put his shoulder to the cross, trying to lift it from the hole. It rose an inch or two, then slammed back down into its resting place. "We have to get him down!" he shouted. "He can't last much longer!"

"I can't," the brown-haired woman said, sobbing as if her heart would break. "I am not strong enough to save him."

"Nor am I," the second echoed.

"Nor I," said the third. "Besides, what will become of us if his executioner returns?"

They gravitated toward each other, circling the cross and watching, their hands covering their faces as they mourned. The man struggled with the cross twice more, then looked upward, to where Phoebe floated above them. "Why don't you help us?" he yelled, shaking his fist at the sky. "Don't you care that he's dying?"

Together, she urged, but again her voice was silent. *Do it together.*

Suddenly the man turned his eyes from the sky overhead to the women around him. "Come on! None of us can do it alone, but if we join forces—"

The women stopped crying. They gathered together at the foot of the cross and reached out to find a handhold on the blood-soaked beam. With a mighty heave, the four of them lifted the cross and laid it on the side of the hill, then wrenched the spikes free and released the boy.

But Phoebe feared they had come too late. An almost-full moon had risen over the eastern ridge, illuminating the child's pallid face in a blue-white light. His eyes were shut, his limbs limp and lifeless.

The brown-haired woman, the first to appear from the forest, sat on the ground and cradled the boy in her lap. A living Pietà in the moonlight. Madonna with her crucified son.

The man ripped off his shirt, and while the women tore it into strips and bandaged the boy's hands and feet, he leaned down over the child and began to breathe into his lungs. One breath. Then two. A third—

The boy's chest rose and fell. He stirred and opened his eyes.

Phoebe gasped. She felt the breath go into her own lungs, felt warm lips pressing against her own. But when she opened her eyes, no one was there.

14

The Revelation

On Monday morning, Phoebe was stirring eggs in the big iron skillet when she heard slow clumping footfalls on the back stairs. Lewis came into the kitchen, dragging his feet as if the weight of the universe lay on his bony little shoulders. He hugged Phoebe around the waist from behind, then climbed onto a tall stool and sat there, watching, as she finished cooking breakfast.

"Could you check the toast for me?" Phoebe gave him a kiss on the cheek and pointed to the broiler beneath the gas oven. "It should be done by now. Use the potholder, and be careful."

Lewis took a quilted potholder from the countertop, opened the lower oven door, and slid the pan of toast out from under the flame. Phoebe watched him over her shoulder. It was perfect—just like Gram used to make, with the butter melted and the edges crispy brown. A wave of nostalgia washed over her as the scent reached her nostrils.

"Where's Father?" Lewis asked.

Phoebe turned to see Lewis examining the two place settings on the kitchen table. He was frowning, his wiry little body tensed from head to foot. "Gone to work early, apparently. I didn't see him, but his dirty breakfast dishes were on the table when I came down."

The furrow of tension between Lewis's eyes vanished. His countenance brightened, and he exhaled a sigh of what had to be relief. Phoebe's gut twisted into a knot. *No six-year-old boy should have to live in terror of encountering his own father at the breakfast table.*

Phoebe scooped the scrambled eggs onto a small oval platter, arranged bacon strips around the perimeter, and retrieved a jar of strawberry jam from the icebox. Lewis had already put the toast on a plate and settled himself at the table.

"Looks great," he said. He held out a hand to her as she took the seat across from him. "You ask the blessing—and make it quick. I'm starving."

She clasped his little hand in hers and bowed her head, racking her brain for an appropriate prayer. "Thank you, Dear God, for this food, and for this new day," she said. "May it strengthen and sustain us. Give us wisdom and courage for all you call us to do, and keep us safe in your loving care. Amen."

When she raised her head, Lewis was staring at her as if she had been speaking Swahili. "What?" she asked.

"I don't know. That was just—well, different from the usual

blessing." He scooped eggs onto his plate and loaded a slice of toast with the bright red jam. "Are you OK?"

Phoebe smiled and put two pieces of bacon onto his plate next to the eggs. "Sure. I'm fine." But as she thought about the prayer, she realized it hadn't really come from her conscious mind. It seemed to emanate from some deeper place, some unknown source. *Give us wisdom and courage.* She hadn't really meant to say that—it just came out, as if it was a prayer that needed to be uttered. And it was, now that she thought about it, exactly what she needed.

Wisdom to know how to do what she had to do, and courage to make herself do it.

Today was May 9. Four days from today was Great-Aunt Phoebe's graduation day—and the last day of her life. Only four days left to make a difference.

When Phoebe thought about it, her plan was patently absurd. This wasn't real, and nothing she could possibly do would change anything. But she was going to do it anyway, she'd decided. She couldn't stand the pressure a moment longer, couldn't just sit idly by and let everyone around her believe in the myth of their perfect family. She was tired of fronts and falsehoods. Today, as soon as she could get them all together, she was going to tell Jonathan and Ethyle and Mildred.

All of it. Father's drinking. His mistreatment of Lewis. Her own fears.

She hadn't been able to get the nightmare out of her mind.

There was no question what it meant. Little Lewis was bleeding, dying—at least figuratively. By herself, she couldn't do anything to stop it, but perhaps together the four of them could intervene on Lewis's behalf.

And she had concluded that she had nothing to lose in telling the truth. After all, this whole experience was a dream— a very vivid dream, but a dream nevertheless. If no one believed her, she would be no worse off. Eventually she would reawaken and be back in her old life.

But maybe they would believe her. Maybe they would still love her and support her. It might not make any difference in Lewis's life in the long run, but at least she would have done everything she could.

~

A knock at the back door roused Phoebe from her reverie. She turned from the sink to see Jonathan's blond head poking through the doorway. "Must be nice to be a lady of leisure on a Monday morning, finished with exams and still nearly a week to go until graduation. May I come in?"

"Of course."

"Where's Lewis?"

"He went to the park to play ball with some of his friends." She laughed. "Now that school's out, he's up at the crack of dawn. We finished breakfast an hour ago, and as you see, I'm still dawdling over the dishes. Want a cup of coffee? I made a fresh pot."

"Coffee? Since when did you start drinking coffee?" He grinned at her and came into the kitchen.

Phoebe mentally kicked herself. Great-Aunt Phoebe wasn't twenty-five with a master's degree—she was barely eighteen, still a senior in high school. If Phoebe intended to play this role, she had to remember who she was supposed to be.

"Well, I . . ." She dried her hands and opened the icebox, pretending to look inside. "How about orange juice? Or milk? I have both."

"I'll take the coffee."

She poured a cup from the enamel pot on the back of the stove and handed it to him. He sat down at the table and stared at the cup, chuckling.

"What's wrong?"

"Nothing," he said. "I'm just waiting."

Phoebe frowned. "Waiting for what?"

"For cream and sugar. You know I can't stand this stuff black."

She stifled a sigh and retrieved the sugar bowl and creamer. "Sorry. I wasn't thinking."

Jonathan put in two lumps of sugar and a dollop of cream. He stirred the coffee thoughtfully. "Seems you have a lot on your mind lately."

Phoebe nodded.

"Why don't you sit down and tell me about it?"

She shook her head. "Not yet. I mean, I will. I want to. But I need to do it all at once. Mildred and Ethyle are coming over at ten, and if you don't mind, I'll wait and talk to all of you at the same time." She looked at the clock over the stove; it was nine-forty.

Jonathan sipped his coffee. "At least sit down. You're making me nervous."

Phoebe perched on the chair at right angles to Jonathan and watched as he drank his coffee. The clock ticked loudly in the silence.

At last Jonathan broke the tension. "Have you thought any more about what I asked you?"

"About what?"

"About running away with me to Fiji and living a life of debauchery."

"No," Phoebe said absently, "I'm afraid I've had other things on my mind."

Jonathan threw back his head and laughed. "Phoebe, you're not listening."

"Yes, I am."

"Then, what did I say?"

"You asked me if—" Phoebe faltered. "All right, you win. I wasn't listening."

"I asked—or intended to ask—if you have thought any more about getting married." At her blank stare, he went on, "You know, you and me. Married. Husband and wife. For better or worse. Does any of this ring a bell? I *did* propose, you recall."

Despite her best intentions, Phoebe's eyes filled with tears. "I remember. I just can't answer you right now." She took a deep breath and fought for control. "After you hear what I have to say, you may want to withdraw the offer."

Jonathan leaned forward and captured her hand in his. "What is it, Phoebe? What's going on?"

She was saved from having to respond by the sound of voices and a clatter of feet on the back porch steps. Two young women swept into the kitchen with a flurry of chatter and laughter. "Mildred, I can't believe you would have the nerve—"

Phoebe stared at them. She had talked to them both on the telephone, asking them to come over. But until this moment, she had only seen them in photographs from the Memory Book. She recognized them immediately—Mildred, tall and dark-haired and composed; Ethyle, bubbly and cheerful, with dazzling red hair. The resemblance to Naomi and Krista was minimal, and yet Phoebe was taken aback by an eerie sense of déjà vu.

As soon as they caught sight of Phoebe's face, they fell silent.

"What's happened? Did somebody die?"

Phoebe thought of the nightmare, the boy impaled upon the cross, and she shuddered. "Nobody died. Have a seat."

They sat around the kitchen table and exchanged greetings with Jonathan while Phoebe busied herself with serving coffee and juice and a platter of apple turnovers. She needed time to compose herself, to think what to do next. Now that the moment was upon her, she wasn't sure she had the fortitude to reveal the truth to them.

"Courage and wisdom," she whispered to herself under her

breath. The reminder bolstered her resolve. She quit fluttering around the kitchen, sat down at the table, and folded her hands in front of her.

"This is very awkward," she said. "I'm not quite sure where to begin." Her mind raced back through the diary pages she had read. Great-Aunt Phoebe had admitted to withdrawing from her friends, and seemed to have regretted it. Maybe she should start with an apology. "I haven't been a very good friend to any of you lately, and I ask for your forgiveness."

No one said a word. They just stared at her, waiting.

At last Mildred spoke up. "We have noticed that you've been—well, not quite yourself," she said cautiously.

Phoebe stifled a laugh. If they only knew how *not herself* she really was. She bit her lip and continued. "Yes. I've not quite been myself. I've been preoccupied and inattentive, and I'm sorry for that. But there's more to it than that—much more. I've been avoiding being honest with the three of you, and that's not how I want to be with my best friends."

She paused and looked at them. Jonathan, with his fair hair and guileless blue eyes, his face filled with an expression of love and concern. Ethyle, the social butterfly, with a sprinkling of freckles across her nose and that wild red hair curling around her temples. Mildred, the serious one of the group, her dark eyes darting from one face to another. They all loved her—or rather, loved Great-Aunt Phoebe. And still, what she was about to tell them seemed an enormous risk.

"When Mother died," Phoebe said, staring down at the tabletop and summoning up every detail she could recall of what she had read in her great-aunt's diary, "you all know that I took on the care of Lewis. I didn't resent it. I love him, and in many ways he has been my last link to Mother. But once she was gone, things began to change."

"Of course things changed," Ethyle chimed in. "And you've done a marvelous job taking on that responsibility. We all admire you, the way your family has gone on."

"You won't admire this family so much," Phoebe countered, "when you hear what I have to say. After Mother's death, Father began—well, he began to drink. A great deal. Every night, he would sequester himself in his study, and many mornings I would find him still in there, asleep on the couch in the clothes he had worn the previous day."

"A lot of people do uncharacteristic things when they're in mourning," Mildred said. "Your father is a good man, Phoebe."

"My father is a drunk," Phoebe said bluntly. "I've covered up for him, made excuses for him. I've pretended that everything was fine. But it's not fine. It's horrible. I have to tell someone, and you're the only people I really trust." The tears began to build up again, and Phoebe struggled to blink them back. How could this be so difficult, when it wasn't even her own life she was talking about?

Jonathan scooted his chair closer and laid a comforting hand over her clenched fists. "Go on, Phoebe. We're listening."

"Ever since Mother's death, Father's anger began building

up. At first he would only take it out on himself, drinking himself into a stupor. But then he began to take it out on my brother." She paused, summoning her resolve. "He beats Lewis. And not just a spanking, to discipline him. He straps him with a belt for the least little infraction, or for no reason at all. He leaves bruises and welts on Lewis's legs and back. Sometimes he draws blood. Lewis tries to please him, but with Father, that's impossible. And the worst of it is, I feel as if God has abandoned me. I try to pray, but I don't feel as if my prayers are being heard. I don't know what to do. I'm afraid for Lewis, afraid he—"

Phoebe couldn't go any further. She couldn't stand to look at them, couldn't bear to see their expressions of pity or repulsion. She hid her face in her hands and began to weep. Silence descended around her, broken only by the ticking of the clock and the ragged sound of her own sobbing. What must they think of her, breaking down like this? She tried to regain control of herself, and yet the floodgates had been opened, and she couldn't stop the tears. There would be no shutting them until the full force of her anger and pain had been expelled. Even as she wept, Phoebe realized that the tears weren't all for Lewis, or for her great-aunt. She was crying, at least in part, for herself—for her own irreclaimable childhood, for all the lost years, all the fears, all the agony she could never forget.

The silence stretched on. Then Phoebe began to feel something. The weight of a hand on her shoulder. Arms encircling her. Something warm and wet dripping into her hair.

She looked up. Mildred and Ethyle were standing on each side of her, their arms around her shoulders, and around each other. Jonathan was embracing her from behind, his head leaning forward. No one said a word, but all eyes were rimmed with red, all faces streaked with tears.

"God has not abandoned you," Jonathan whispered at last. "We're here."

15

A Different Kind of Family

Phoebe told them everything—at least everything she knew from Great-Aunt Phoebe's journal and what she had gleaned from her own limited experience with Lewis and Father. For more than an hour she sat at the kitchen table with Great-Aunt Phoebe's fiancé and two best friends and poured it all out, unsifted and uncensored. She cried some more, and they cried with her. When she got to the part about the dream of the little boy being crucified by his father, both serious Mildred and flighty Ethyle wept openly. Jonathan's face went as white as his crisp starched shirt.

Remarkably, when it was all over and the tears had dried, Phoebe felt strangely liberated, as if she had vicariously opened up her own soul rather than simply recounted what she had learned of her great-aunt's feelings from the diary. It was a bit like the catharsis of watching a Shakespearean tragedy, except that she was a participant, an actor on the stage instead of a viewer in the audience. Releasing those pent-up emotions frightened her a little, but she soon discovered that she had no reason to be afraid. Her friends understood.

"Don't you see?" Jonathan said at last. "Your dream gives us the answer—or part of the answer. None of us can do it alone, but together we can make a difference."

Phoebe smiled—an action that hurt a little, given her puffy face and swollen eyelids. She probably looked a wreck, and yet Jonathan was gazing at her as if she were the most beautiful creature on the face of the earth. He had said the magic word without even realizing it: *us.* They were in this *together,* all of them. Suddenly she felt less alone than she had ever felt in her life.

"So what do we do?" Mildred, all business, planted her hands palm-down on the table and looked around the group.

"I believe I've already proposed a solution," Jonathan said quietly. The expression of love in his eyes generated a quiver of response in Phoebe's heart, even though she tried to remind herself that the look was for Great-Aunt Phoebe, not for herself.

"What solution?" Ethyle took the last apple turnover from the platter and bit into it.

"I've asked Phoebe to marry me," he said. "And to bring Lewis to live with us." He smiled into Phoebe's eyes. "The offer still stands, but I have yet to receive an answer."

Ethyle inhaled sharply and choked on the turnover. Her eyes

began to water, and she coughed until Mildred hammered her on the back to make her stop. "Marriage?" she spluttered. "You've talked about marriage?"

"That's wonderful," Mildred put in. "You two are perfect for each other."

Phoebe barely heard the commotion of Ethyle's choking or Mildred's affirmation. Everything around her faded as she watched Jonathan's face. "Are you sure?" She searched his gaze, looking for some sign of pity or duty or hesitancy, and found none. "Marriage would mean a radical change in your plans for the future. Taking on both a wife and a six-year-old child would entail quite a responsibility."

"And I'm quite a responsible person," he countered. "Yes, I'm sure. Absolutely certain."

"But what about college? The Farm School? Learning photography?"

Jonathan chuckled. "It almost sounds as if you're looking desperately for a back door, an excuse not to say yes. For your information, I have some money saved, and I can work part-time and still finish my degree." He leaned back and folded his arms across his chest. "Next argument."

Phoebe shook her head. "There is no next argument. If you're certain . . ." She took a deep breath and exhaled heavily. Suddenly she knew, without knowing how she knew, what Great-Aunt Phoebe would do. "The answer is yes. But not until after graduation."

He grinned broadly, then the expression faded and his brow furrowed into a frown. "What about Lewis? Could he accept me as a stepfather—or as a big brother?"

"Open your eyes, Jonathan," Phoebe said. "He already adores you. You're practically a brother to him now. He'll be thrilled."

"Then it's settled. Except for one thing." He reached into his vest pocket and pulled out a ring, a small diamond in a gold setting. "I've been carrying this around for weeks. I hope it fits." He slid the ring onto her left hand and pressed her palm to his lips. "Now it's official. Not exactly the kind of romantic setting I had envisioned for such a moment, but it will do." He leaned across the table and kissed her—a slow, lingering kiss. When he drew back, his eyes were sparkling with unshed tears.

Mildred and Ethyle laughed and cheered. Phoebe felt herself blush. "Do you plan to do this often?" she asked. "Kiss me in public and embarrass me in front of our friends?"

He grinned. "As often as possible."

The excited chatter around the table went on for a few minutes as the four of them talked about dates and times and what kind of wedding they should plan. But when they got around to the subject of living arrangements, Mildred suddenly went silent.

"Wait a moment," she said when they had quieted down. "What do we do in the meantime, before the wedding? If your father finds out—"

Phoebe's heart sank. "He'll beat both Lewis and me senseless, probably, and find a way to stop me from going through with this wedding." Reluctantly she pulled the engagement ring from her finger and handed it back to Jonathan. "I can't take the chance that Father will see this. You'd better keep it for now, at least until I've found a way to get out of here."

He nodded somberly and put the ring back into his pocket. "Mildred's right. We need to figure out a plan for the interim."

"Phoebe and Lewis could come and stay with me until after graduation," Mildred offered. "My parents wouldn't mind. Then the two of you could elope—provided you take us along."

Jonathan made a face. "I assume you mean for the wedding, not the honeymoon."

"Oh no, we assumed we'd go on the honeymoon, too." Ethyle giggled and winked at Phoebe.

"But how could we explain it to your parents, Mildred, without telling them the whole story?" Phoebe asked.

"Why not tell them?" Mildred said. "It seems to me that the high-and-mighty Mr. Lange ought to have to face the consequences of everyone knowing what he has done."

Jonathan shook his head. "I agree that he deserves whatever he gets, but we have to think about Lewis. We don't want him hurt any more, and it would shame him if everyone around him knew what he'd been through. I think for now we have to keep this to ourselves."

Phoebe's mind reeled. This situation was much more complicated than she had expected. If this were 2001 instead of

1927, one call to the Department of Social Services would serve to remove Lewis to a safe place and put Father on notice, if not in jail. But in 1927, people still held to the view that children were essentially property, and that parents had the right to "discipline" them as they pleased. No public official would take Lewis's side against his father's.

"Still," Jonathan was saying, "we need to find some way to let Mr. Lange know that we know. Perhaps he won't be so quick to strike if he feels people are looking over his shoulder."

"I'd rather not provoke him if I can avoid it," Phoebe objected. "He'd take it out on Lewis—and maybe on me."

Jonathan rose to his feet, and a transformation came over him unlike anything Phoebe had ever seen. His jaw clenched, and the veins on his neck stood out like wire cables. He was a small man, wiry and compact, but at that moment he seemed to grow taller and more muscular right before her eyes. "If he dares to lay a hand on either of you, he'll have to answer to me. And believe me, I will not be in a mood for rational conversation."

Phoebe felt herself flush as a wave of love and appreciation welled up within her. "We'll be all right, Jonathan. Graduation is less than a week away. I'll have a talk with Lewis this afternoon. In the meantime, we'll keep a low profile and try to stay out of Father's way."

With a grunt of assent, Jonathan dropped back into his chair. "All right. I suppose that's for the best. But be careful. And if anything happens, you will call me immediately?"

"Of course I will." Phoebe reached out and squeezed his hand. "Thank you. Thank you all. I was afraid to tell you this, afraid of what your response might be."

"Afraid we would abandon you?" Mildred said. "Ridiculous."

"Absolutely absurd," Ethyle chimed in. "What are friends for, if not to support each other during difficult times?"

"We'll get through this, you'll see." Jonathan gripped her hand tightly. "You'll graduate, we'll be married, and this will all be put behind us, just a painful memory from the past." He bit his lower lip and narrowed his eyes. "If I have anything to say about it, my darling, nothing will ever hurt you again."

Phoebe forced a smile. Her great-aunt was truly a fortunate woman, to have friends who loved her so much, who were willing to stand by her. Something Jonathan had said earlier came back to her, a phrase she now saw in a new light: *"God has not abandoned you. We're here."*

She lifted her eyes to the ceiling and breathed a silent prayer of gratitude.

~

Phoebe spent the rest of the afternoon cleaning the house and cooking a pot roast with carrots and onions and potatoes. She wasn't about to do anything that might displease Father and set him off—not now, when liberation truly seemed a possibility.

As she dusted in the parlor and beat out the rugs on the clothesline, Phoebe questioned why she was doing all this. If her presence here wasn't real, then any improvement she managed to make in Lewis's situation would be temporary, at best. And yet she found herself so immersed in the role that she sometimes actually *felt* like Great-Aunt Phoebe. She had already come to regard Lewis as her little brother instead of her grandfather, and her feelings for Jonathan Barksdale went astonishingly deep. She could still feel the sensation of that engagement ring on her hand, even for the brief few moments she had worn it. Her mind kept bringing her back to the look of love and longing in his eyes in that instant when he had slipped it onto her finger and leaned forward to kiss her. A warm, wonderful kiss, full of promise and hope for the future.

But there was no future for Great-Aunt Phoebe. In four days, she would die. Her dreams for a life with Jonathan and for raising little Lewis to manhood would crash into nothingness, trapped in the mangled wreckage of an automobile accident.

Phoebe exhaled heavily and tried to push the depressing thought to the back of her mind. So be it. She couldn't change the inevitable. But perhaps she could make a difference, even a minuscule one, in the meantime.

At the stroke of six, just as she was taking the roast out of the oven, Father arrived home from work. He looked around, then stalked into the kitchen, obviously in a sour mood.

"You cleaned the house." It was an accusation, not a question.

"Yes," Phoebe answered. "I know you like things orderly."

"Was anyone here today? Were you entertaining those . . . those *friends* of yours without my permission?" He furrowed his heavy brows and scowled at her.

Phoebe put on her brightest smile. "I made your favorite dinner, Father. Smells delicious, doesn't it?"

"Don't change the subject. Was someone here, or not? That good-for-nothing Barksdale boy, perhaps?"

"I thought you liked Jonathan."

"His father came into the bank today, telling a cock-and-bull story about his son buying an engagement ring for some girl he was sweet on. Let me see your hand."

He grabbed Phoebe's left wrist and twisted it hard. She winced at the pain, but sent up a silent prayer of thanks that she had given back the ring. "See, Father? No ring."

"Let's keep it that way." He dropped her hand and slammed a fist down on the counter. "That boy has failure written all over him. His father manages the movie theater, did you know that? Little more than a glorified janitor. And the son sweeps up the floors at night."

Phoebe felt her stomach knot with anger. Father barely knew Jonathan, had no idea of his dreams and ambitions. And yet she had to keep a lid on her temper—for Lewis's sake, if not for her own.

"Father, come and sit down. I've made a nice dinner; we'll eat in the dining room. I'll call Lewis, and—"

"Don't bother. Make me a plate, and I'll take it into my study. I've got work to do." He turned on his heel and stalked away.

You've got drinking to do, Phoebe thought as she watched his retreating back. But she kept silent.

~

Lewis, energized from his day outdoors in the sunshine and fresh air, ate two helpings of roast beef and three biscuits. Phoebe insisted that he have at least one serving of the carrots, too, and listened with interest as he told her about the ball game.

"At first they put me out in right field, 'cause the guy who was our captain—they call him Bruiser; he's eight and real bossy—he was sure I was too little to be any good," he said around a mouthful of potatoes and gravy. "Didn't even want me to play. But then I made a real good catch, and threw the ball in all the way to home almost." He grinned and, for a fraction of a second, almost looked like a normal, happy little boy. "So the next inning, Bruiser brought me in to play shortstop. And guess what?"

Phoebe leaned forward and ruffled his hair. "What?"

"I caught a grounder and tagged second and threw it to first and made a double play."

"That's wonderful, Lewis!"

"Yeah," he said. "'Course, the kid who was batting tripped on his shoelace and fell down before he got to first, but I got him out anyway."

"Could I come watch you play sometime?"

Lewis ducked his head, and his ears turned bright red. "Aw, I don't know. The big boys might make fun of me if my sister came hanging around." But he beamed up at her, obviously pleased that she'd ask.

"OK, I'll stay away. Do you want some more roast beef?"

"No, thanks. I'm stuffed." He leaned back in his chair. "But it was real good."

Phoebe got up, cleared the dishes from the table, and began putting away the leftovers. "I don't suppose you have room for apple pie, then."

"I always have room for pie."

She cut a large slice for him and a slightly smaller one for herself, then sat back down across from him. "Lewis, I have something to talk to you about, but it needs to be a secret, just between you and me."

He looked up, his fork paused in midair. "A secret?"

"Yes. And you have to promise not to tell anyone."

"I promise."

"How would you feel about going to live somewhere else?"

Lewis screwed up his face in confusion. "Somewhere else?"

"Yes. A place where"—she threw a glance in the direction of Father's study—"where you'd never have to worry about being hurt again."

He dropped the fork onto his plate and pushed the half-eaten pie toward the center of the table. For a minute or two he dug his fingernail into the woodgrain of the tabletop. When he raised his head again, his eyes were filled with tears. "You mean without you?"

"Oh no, Lewis," she said hurriedly. "You wouldn't be leaving me. You'd be coming to live with me. With me and Jonathan."

He frowned and swiped at the unshed tears. "I don't understand."

Phoebe leaned forward and lowered her voice to a whisper. "Jonathan has asked me to marry him. And he wants you to come and live with us. Forever."

The storm clouds passed from Lewis's face, and the sun came out so quickly that Phoebe had difficulty tracking the transformation. "Without Father?"

"Yes, without Father. Just you and me and Jonathan. He would be like a father to you. Or like a big brother. We'd be a family, the three of us. Just a different kind of family."

Lewis jumped out of his chair and began dancing up and down. "Yes. *Yes*. YES! When? Can we go now, today?"

"Not so fast, buddy. We've got some planning to do. And you've got to help me."

He sat down and grew serious. "What do you want me to do?"

"First, I want you to keep this to yourself. You mustn't tell *anyone*, understand?"

Lewis nodded solemnly and made an X across his heart. "What else?"

"Well, we don't have everything planned, but I think this is how it will work. We can't do anything until after graduation. Then, probably the week after, Jonathan and I will elope—"

"What's *lope* mean?" Lewis interrupted.

"It's *e-lope*. It means to run away and get married. You can come with us for the wedding, but then afterwards, you'll have to come back with Mildred and Ethyle, and stay at Mildred's house while Jonathan and I go on a short honeymoon."

"A honeymoon?"

Phoebe stifled a laugh and racked her brain to figure out how to explain a honeymoon to a six-year-old. "It's what married people do. Kind of a tradition. After the wedding, they go away for a few days, just the two of them."

Lewis thought about that for a minute, and Phoebe could almost see the little gears turning in his mind. She braced herself for a protest at the idea of being left behind. But the resistance came in a different form.

"Can I stay with Ethyle instead of Mildred?"

"I suppose so. Why?"

"'Cause Ethyle's more fun. Mildred'll make me eat all sorts of yucky things, like vegetables."

Phoebe suppressed a giggle. "I make you eat vegetables. I made you eat carrots tonight."

"That's different. You're my sister."

"OK," Phoebe sighed. "Ethyle it is. I suppose it won't hurt for a few days."

"And then you'll come back, and we'll live together in a different house?"

"Yes. I'm not sure where just yet. Jonathan will take care of that."

"But you *will* come back? You won't just leave me? You promise?"

The desperation in his voice tugged at Phoebe's heart. "Why would you even ask such a question? I would never leave you."

"Mommy did."

Tears stung Phoebe's eyes. She got up, went around the table, and stood behind Lewis, embracing him in a fierce hug and kissing the top of his head. He smelled like sunshine and dirt and little-boy sweat and soda crackers. "Mommy died, Lewis. She didn't have a choice. She never would have left you if she'd had a choice."

"I know," he sighed. "I don't remember her, but I still think about her sometimes and wish she was here." He wriggled out of her arms and turned around to face her. "Was it my fault she died?"

"No, Lewis, it wasn't your fault. Did someone tell you it was?"

He lowered his eyes. "Father says so sometimes, when he's real mad."

Phoebe grasped him by the arms and looked into his face. "Father's wrong. Father's wrong about a lot of things. Mother's death was terrible, but you were the blessing that came out of it."

"Really, Phoebe?" He brightened a little. "I was the blessing?"

She gathered the thin little body close. "You were, and you are, Lewis. A blessing. Straight from the hand of God."

He snuggled in to her and sighed. "And soon there'll be another blessing. You and me and Jonathan. A family. A different kind of family."

"That's right," Phoebe said. And silently, in her heart, she raised the urgent plea: *Please, God, let it be so.*

16

No Greater Love

Three days passed without incident. Father divided his time between his office at the bank and his study at home. Phoebe rarely saw him except in passing, but the few times he drew close, she could smell the liquor on his breath, even at midday. His hooded eyes seethed with a dark and inscrutable anger, calling up images of a volcano about to blow.

Phoebe kept her distance, kept the peace—and made certain Lewis did the same.

The boy, on the other hand, had never seemed so happy, so relaxed. So . . . normal. His narrow little face glowed with the joy of his wonderful secret, and his step lightened. When the two of them were alone, his anticipation spilled out in childish chatter and a dancing, lilting laugh.

Phoebe was putting together a stew when he raced into the kitchen from the front parlor. "To-mor-row is grad-u-a-tion," he announced in a gleeful singsong, bouncing on his toes. "You know what that means."

Phoebe's stomach lurched as the thought assailed her: it meant that Great-Aunt Phoebe was about to die. *But maybe not,* another part of her mind argued. *Maybe things have changed, will change. Maybe—*

She pushed the thought aside. "It means I have to press my dress and go over my speech tonight."

"And what else?" He leaned over and snatched a cookie from a plate on the counter.

"What else? Why, I haven't the faintest idea." She winked at him.

He lowered his voice to a whisper. "We're leaving first thing Saturday morning, right? For the lopement?"

"That's right. We'll slip out of the house while you-know-who is sleeping. Pack everything you'll want to take with you, because we won't be coming back." Phoebe ruffled his hair. "You can use the big suitcase in the hall closet. But don't leave it out where Father can see it."

"I've already started," he said. "The suitcase is under the bed, and—"

"Lewis!" a voice roared from the front parlor. "LEWIS! Get in here. NOW!"

The wide grin froze in place, and all the color drained out of the boy's cheeks. "Uh-oh."

Phoebe felt her stomach twist into a pretzel. "Just stay put. Take it easy."

A hulking shadow filled the doorway to the kitchen. Phoebe looked up to see Father, his face beet-red, his eyes bleary and bloodshot. In his hands he held a battered baseball bat.

The volcano had erupted.

"You left this on the stairs. I nearly tripped over it. I could have been killed." He brandished the bat in Lewis's face. "How many times have I told you not to leave your toys lying around the house?"

Phoebe stepped forward and took the bat. "I'm sorry, Father. It's my fault. I put it there temporarily, intending to take it to his room the next time I went upstairs. Then I got busy making dinner and never had the chance to put it away."

He didn't look at her, not once. His eyes were focused on the lad. "Your things. Your responsibility. Into my study. Go."

Lewis's shoulders slumped, and he fixed his eyes on the tile of the kitchen floor.

"Father, don't!" Phoebe pleaded. "He's just a boy."

He whirled, and for the first time looked directly into Phoebe's face. A shiver ran through her at the sight of those eyes—cold, flat, soulless. "You stay out of this," he said, punctuating each word with a deliberate pause. Then he turned and followed Lewis in the direction of the study.

Phoebe stood rooted to the spot and watched them go. They had been close . . . so close. Two more days, and—

Then she came to herself. What was she thinking? She couldn't give up hope now. And she wasn't about to stand idly by and let Father beat poor Lewis again. No matter what it cost.

She turned the heat off under the stew and bolted for the other room.

~

The study door was closed. Beyond the thick oak she could hear Father yelling, although she couldn't make out the words. Then the voice ceased. A deathly silence descended.

Phoebe stood there, hesitating for a moment. Father's voice came again, more quietly this time. She pressed her ear to the door.

"Answer me!" she heard Father's muffled voice say. "What did you say?"

"Nothing." Lewis responded, his voice faint and trembly. She could tell he had been crying.

"Don't *nothing* me, boy. You'll tell me the truth or I'll beat it out of you."

Phoebe was just about to open the door when she heard Lewis's voice again, this time infused with a determination far beyond his years. "You can beat me now, but it will be the last time."

"What does that mean?"

Phoebe held her breath. *No,* she begged silently. *Lewis, no.*

But her prayer was to no avail. Her blood chilled when she heard him say, "We're leaving. Me and Phoebe and Jonathan." A pause, then, "That's what I said. Jonathan knows what you do to me. *Everybody* knows."

She heard the whap of leather against skin, heard Lewis's cry. Before the strap could fall again, Phoebe opened the door, rushed into the room, and caught the belt midair on the back swing.

"Stop it!" she demanded. "Stop it right now!"

Jerked off-balance by her force pulling against the belt, Father wheeled around toward her. "You!"

"Yes, me," Phoebe answered. She stared defiantly into his eyes, facing down that mask of rage with a boldness that came from somewhere else, some reserve deep inside her that she had never tapped before.

He turned on her, spewing out a string of curses. Lewis escaped to the corner behind the desk. Out of the corner of her eye, Phoebe could see him cowering there, watching.

She snatched the strap out of Father's hand. "You will not do this. Ever again."

"Give me the belt."

"No."

"He is my son, and I will discipline him as I see fit."

"Discipline? You terrorize an innocent child, and you call it discipline?" Phoebe shook her head. "What would Mother think?"

It was the wrong thing to say, and she knew it immediately. His face went white, and his eyes narrowed to slits. He advanced on her before she could react, and the back of his hand smashed across her cheek.

Phoebe staggered, stunned with the pain. Lights flashed behind her eyes, and before she could gather her wits, he hit her again. This time she felt her lip split and her mouth fill with blood. He was upon her, pressing her against the wall, his hands around her throat. The sickening odor of whiskey surrounded her like a noxious cloud. Somewhere in the distance she could hear Lewis sobbing, shouting. She scratched at her father's hands, clawing him, trying to break free. But it was no use. He was too strong.

She couldn't breathe, couldn't see. She was dying. She could feel it. Lewis's voice sounded further and further away. Everything went dim.

Then, suddenly, air rushed into her lungs. She sank down against the wall, her chest heaving as she struggled to draw in a breath. Father had let her go.

No. Someone had pulled him off. She squinted against the pain and tried to see. A figure, shorter than Father by a head and smaller by fifty pounds, had him by the arm, blocking a blow. A fist connected with Father's jaw, and he went down, sprawled unconscious on the Persian rug.

Arms went around Phoebe then, holding her. A hand supported her head underneath, cradling her gently, as if she were a baby. Lewis's face appeared, peering down upon her from above. And then, haloed by the overhead light, a blond head. An angel.

"Darling, it's me. Jonathan. Are you all right?"

She nodded groggily and tried to speak, but her tongue was stuck to the roof of her mouth and wouldn't move. He pressed a handkerchief to the split place on her lip, and she winced with pain.

"You came," she mumbled at last. "How did you know to come?"

"I didn't know," he said, kissing her forehead and stroking her hair. "I just came, that's all."

~

By the time Father regained consciousness, the sheriff was on the scene. Two deputies handcuffed him and hustled him to the waiting police car. He did not go quietly. Phoebe could still hear him screaming obscenities and yelling about his right to discipline his own children, even after the front door had closed behind him.

"A couple of nights in jail will sober him up and cool him off," the sheriff said. "You sure you don't need to go to the hospital, Miss?"

Phoebe shook her head. "I'll be fine."

The truth was, she didn't *feel* fine. A huge goose egg had risen up on her cheek. Her right eye was swollen shut, and her lower lip had ballooned to three times its normal size. Her whole body felt stiff and bruised, as if she had been run over by a herd of buffaloes.

But she was alive. Lewis was safe. And Jonathan sat in the love seat beside her with his arm around her and a worried look on his face.

"I'm all right, Jonathan," she assured him. "Really I am."

"If I hadn't been here, he would have killed you."

The sheriff settled himself on the edge of the desk and twirled his hat in his hands. "That was a very brave and stupid thing to do, Missy. Your beau here is right—you could have been killed."

"Or my brother could have been." She looked up at Lewis, who was standing beside the love seat, and reached out to take his hand. "I wasn't about to let that happen, no matter what Father did to me."

"Like I said," the sheriff repeated. "Brave and stupid." He ruffled Lewis's hair. "You got yourself quite a sister there, little man."

Lewis ducked his head. "I know."

Phoebe touched a finger to the bruise on her cheek. "What happens now?"

"Well," the sheriff went on, "whipping a child may not be a crime, but assault with intent to kill is. Your daddy will be in jail for a few days, until the judge can set a court date. Then, if he can make bail, he'll be released until he comes to trial. But that won't happen until Monday at the earliest."

Monday. By Monday they would all be free. Phoebe started to smile, then thought better of it when the least movement caused excruciating pain in her lip.

"I must look a wreck," she said. "And I'm supposed to deliver the valedictory address tomorrow night."

Jonathan brushed a stray lock of hair off her forehead. "You look beautiful." When she glared at him, he amended his comment. "Well, maybe just a bit the worse for wear. But with a little powder here and there, you'll be good as new."

She gazed into his eyes. "Why *did* you come, Jonathan? You couldn't have foreseen what was going to happen here tonight. How did you know I needed you?"

"Did I have some kind of message from on high, you mean, some inner compulsion to be in the right place at the right time?" He shrugged. "I'm afraid it was nothing so mysterious as all that. I didn't know you needed me. I needed you." He smiled and squeezed her hand. "I missed you. I wanted to see the woman I love. That's all."

Phoebe suspected it was more than that. Much more. But for now, it was enough.

17

The Pearl of Great Price

Preparing for an elopement, Phoebe discovered, was infinitely easier with Father out of the way. In fact, everything was simpler with him gone. Subconsciously, of course, she had been aware of the sense of dread that pervaded the house, but she had not perceived how much the tension had affected her. Now that the pressure had been lifted, she realized that she had been walking on eggshells, her whole body and soul clenched for the inevitable blowup.

This morning she had awakened not with apprehension but with a light heart and an exhilarating sense of anticipation that she could only identify as hope. The feeling reminded her of that familiar moment on the trip from Atlanta to Asheville when she would crest the top of the hill just beyond Traveler's Rest and see the Blue Ridge Mountains rising in layered splendor in the distance. In that instant, all tautness drained from her body. Her jaw relaxed, and her pulse rate slowed, as if a tranquilizer had been injected directly into her veins.

Humming to herself, she went about the business of packing and cleaning and getting ready for the trip. Tonight at 8:00 was graduation. Tomorrow morning, she and Jonathan and Lewis would drive to Gatlinburg for a small wedding in a little chapel overlooking the Smoky Mountains. Mildred and Ethyle would follow in a second car, and after the wedding, they would bring Lewis back to Asheville while Jonathan and Phoebe stayed on for a brief honeymoon.

Before Father's arrest, Phoebe had been apprehensive that he might find Lewis at Ethyle's house and try to take him by force. But now, with Father safely locked away in jail, that fear had been allayed. By Monday, she and Jonathan would be married. Lewis would come to live with them. It was all working out perfectly.

Except for one thing. Today was May 13. The day Great-Aunt Phoebe was supposed to die.

Phoebe had tried not to think about it, had tried to convince herself that it wasn't going to happen. According to Gram, Great-Aunt Phoebe had died in a car wreck on a mountain road. They would be driving no mountain roads tonight. Just a simple, quick trip through town to the auditorium and back again after the ceremony. She could put her mind at ease.

When she had latched her suitcase and set it in the front hallway next to Lewis's, Phoebe went to the kitchen and sat at the table. She had an hour to review the valedictory address she had found in the drawer of Great-Aunt Phoebe's desk, but it lay untouched on the table in front of her. Instead she found herself staring out the window, her mind wandering.

One week ago—or however long it had been in dream-days—she had begun this strange role-play, taking on Great-Aunt Phoebe's life. In that short time, she had fallen in love with little brother Lewis, become engaged to Jonathan, and found in Mildred and Ethyle faithful friends willing to stand with her to confront a problem none of them could have faced alone. She had discovered within herself reserves of love and courage she never knew existed.

And now her old life, her real life, seemed very foreign and far away. She could hardly recognize the trapped, isolated, fearful person she had once been. For months she had resisted the idea of marrying Jake, even though she loved him. She had kept Krista and Naomi at arm's length, certain that if they knew the truth about her, and more recently about her mother's death and her father's crime, they would never see her the same way again. She had been convinced that if she took the risk to be open and unguarded with them, she would end up alone and friendless and totally bereft.

Phoebe wanted to be loved, the way she felt loved and cherished and accepted here, in the dream-world. And yet she had never found the courage to give the significant people in her life the chance to love her.

How had it happened? How had she been able, in playing Great-Aunt Phoebe's part, to take such risks and allow herself to be vulnerable in such unimaginable ways?

The answer came to her in a flash of insight: *Lewis*. In adopting Great-Aunt Phoebe's role, she had taken on the responsibility of protecting an innocent child. Given the choice between safeguarding him and maintaining her walls of self-protection, there was no debate. She had to do what was best for him, even if it meant opening herself to the possibility of rejection. Even if it meant confronting Father and putting her own life in jeopardy.

But that was only a partial answer. The rest of it Phoebe knew instinctively. She had been able to be honest and vulnerable here, in Great-Aunt Phoebe's world, precisely because she had nothing to lose. If she were rejected here, she would eventually awaken as herself and go on. Acting a part involved no great risk. Real life, on the other hand, could be dangerous.

Her thoughts were interrupted when the clock in the front parlor chimed six. Lewis was upstairs taking a bath, and a light dinner was already prepared for the two of them. At seven, Jonathan would be arriving to take the two of them to the commencement ceremonies. She shuffled the papers in front of her and tried to focus on the speech.

Today, as graduating seniors, we set off on a new path, an unexplored way that will take us places we have never been before. We call this ceremony "commencement." It is a completion, certainly, but even more importantly, it is a beginning, a starting place. And although some of us are simply glad to have finished, we must realize that this is not the end. It is merely the first bend in a road that will present to us numerous turns and intersections in the future.

We cannot know what the future holds for us. We hope for happiness, for loving families, for security. But there is more to life than taking the safe way. Life is about risk, about choosing the road less traveled. I must admit that I have not always been good at risk taking. Sometimes I have been afraid to take chances, to embrace the unexpected, to dance on the edge of the cliff. But I want to commit myself to beginning, here and now, the practice of courage, and I invite you to do the same.

Let us not come to the end of our lives only to find that we have never lived. Let us give ourselves with abandon to the future. Let us stand up for what is right, even if it costs all we have. Let us break out of our safe places, breathe fresh air, feel the wind on our faces. Let us become all that our Creator has designed us to be— men and women of faith and daring and undaunted determination.

Let us go forth fearlessly into the unknown, trusting in ourselves and in one another. Let us live with integrity and honor, knowing that we do have and will *have all the reserves of fortitude we need to face whatever life holds for us. Let us be people of principle, people who live by the truth that fills our souls. Above all, let us love freely and hold fast to the friendships we have forged here. Let us give of ourselves to those around us, knowing that love itself is the Pearl of Great Price, worth whatever we spend to possess it.*

Phoebe's eyes focused on the last sentence of her great-aunt's speech. She gingerly touched a fingertip to her split lip and thought about Lewis, and about Jonathan Barksdale, about Ethyle and Mildred. What friendship was theirs, to love Great-Aunt Phoebe so well and risk so much for her? Perhaps for the first time in her life, Phoebe realized, she had seen unconditional love in action. The Pearl of Great Price.

She stacked the pages of the speech neatly, slipped them into a folder, and went upstairs to dress for graduation.

~

Phoebe stood on the stage clutching the podium for support as a wave of cheers and applause crested over her. She had managed to get through Great-Aunt Phoebe's speech with a modicum of grace and self-confidence, and now, as she focused her attention on two faces in the crowd, her heart swelled with pride and gratitude.

Below her, in the third row, Jonathan Barksdale rose to his

feet, clapping madly. Beside him, standing on the chair, Lewis waved his cap in the air and whistled. Phoebe inclined her head, acknowledging the affirmation, and retreated to her seat.

But just as she turned, she caught a glimpse of someone in the shadows, back in the far left corner of the auditorium. A man. Not applauding, but standing there glaring toward the stage, his arms folded across his chest. A memory flitted across her mind—twenty years ago, at Mama's funeral—a man standing off in the distance, hunched against the rain. But this was a different face. A face she knew.

Father.

She was sure of it.

How had he managed to get out of jail so quickly? The sheriff had said it would be Monday, at the very earliest, before he could see a judge and have his bail set. He had pulled some strings, no doubt. A respected banker would have friends who would come to his aid. However he had done it, he was here, and the very sight of him chilled Phoebe to the core.

All the blood drained from her head. She stumbled unsteadily back to her chair on the platform. Behind her, in the second row of graduates, Mildred leaned forward and whispered, "Are you all right?"

But Phoebe had no chance to answer. Mr. Cartledge, the principal, had gone to the podium and was beginning to call the roll of graduates and hand out diplomas.

In a fog, she responded to her name, went forward, and

received Great-Aunt Phoebe's honors. She stood and mouthed words during the singing of the school anthem. When the opening chords of the recessional sounded, she followed the line up the center aisle and out into the hallway.

The other graduates milled around, chatting excitedly as they waited for their families and friends to come out of the auditorium. Phoebe sagged against the wall, her eyes frantically searching every shadowed corner. But Father was nowhere to be seen.

At last Jonathan came around the corner, holding Lewis by the hand. He was grinning like a Cheshire cat until he saw her face. Then his smile faded. "Phoebe, are you ill? You look very pale."

As if out of thin air, Mildred and Ethyle appeared at Phoebe's elbow. "She got sick right after her speech," Mildred said in answer to Jonathan's question. "She went all white and seemed dizzy." She looked at Phoebe. "What happened?"

"Father," Phoebe said.

"He was here?" Jonathan's jaw clenched, and the veins in his neck pulsed. "How did he get out of jail?"

"I have no idea. But he was here. I saw him, standing in the back of the hall. By the time we processed out, he had disappeared."

"What do you suppose he wants?" Ethyle asked.

Phoebe gritted her teeth. "I doubt he simply wanted to hear his darling daughter's valedictory address."

Jonathan took Phoebe's arm. "I think we all know why he came. And what he wants. We have to get out of here."

The tone of his voice frightened Phoebe, and she felt an icy chill climb the back of her neck. "And do what? Just go home, as if nothing has happened?"

"Not a chance." Jonathan shook his head. "I'm getting you out of his reach, now, tonight. We're going to Gatlinburg. Once we're married, he'll have no further claim on you."

"But what about Lewis?"

Jonathan wrapped a protective arm around the boy. "If he tries to get to Lewis, he'll have to come through me first."

"Jonathan, we can't," Phoebe protested. "We don't have any clothes, and it's so late—"

She couldn't tell him the rest—that Great-Aunt Phoebe had died, this very night, in a car wreck on a dark mountain road. Maybe this was her chance. Maybe she could do something, here, now, to keep that particular detail of history from repeating itself.

"Do you have a better idea?"

Phoebe closed her eyes and exhaled heavily. "No."

Mildred had been shifting impatiently from one foot to the other. "You three go on," she said when she could get a word in. "In the morning, Ethyle and I will go by the house and pick up your suitcases. We'll meet you at the chapel."

"What if you run into Father?" Phoebe said.

"Don't worry about us. We'll keep a sharp eye out and stay out of his way. Now go."

Mildred put her arms around Phoebe and drew her into a

ferocious hug. "Everything will be all right," she whispered. "We'll pray for you."

Then Mildred and Ethyle were gone, and Jonathan was hustling Phoebe and Lewis out the door toward the waiting car.

⌒

Even in mid-May, nights in the mountains were cold. Escaping across the state line in an open Model T Roadster was a chilling proposition at best. But Jonathan had the foresight to bring blankets, and now Lewis was bundled up in the rumble seat and Phoebe in the passenger's seat as they negotiated the winding, precarious mountain road north toward Tennessee.

Lewis leaned back in the seat and whooped for joy, grinning as if this was a grand adventure. After a while even Phoebe began to relax a bit. Everything seemed to be going smoothly. Perhaps what she had already done—standing up to Father, agreeing to marry Jonathan—was enough to change the course of this night.

She craned her neck and looked through the windshield. The moon hung over the valley to their left, descending in the west. Above them, a billion stars glittered like diamonds scattered across a velvet sky.

Jonathan shifted gears, removed his glove, and reached out to grasp Phoebe's hand. His touch, warm and reassuring, comforted her, and she squeezed his fingers in response.

"We're going to be all right," he said. "I love you."

Phoebe blinked back tears. "I love you, too."

Lewis let out a loud groan from the backseat. "Are you two going to be mushy and romantic all the way to Gatlinburg?"

Jonathan turned and grinned at him over one shoulder. "Yes." Then his smile faded, and he lowered his voice. "We may have trouble."

Phoebe froze. "What kind of trouble?"

"Look behind us."

Phoebe shifted in the seat and looked. Coming up fast, she could see a pair of headlights. They moved back and forth across the lane, as if the driver was having difficulty controlling his automobile.

"It could be just another late-night traveler," Phoebe said.

"Maybe. Let's hope."

The car gained on them steadily, until its headlights were right on their tail, illuminating Lewis's hair in a silvery beam. Jonathan accelerated around a curve.

"Can you see anything?" he shouted over the roar of the engine.

"No. The lights are too bright."

"Hold on."

Phoebe had ridden in fast cars before, and relatively speaking, the Model T was barely puttering along. But the road had numerous turns and switchbacks. To the right, the mountain rose up in a towering cliff of sheer rock, and to the left, it plunged away into a deep chasm. Each time they veered around a curve,

Jonathan edged closer and closer to the cliff side, until Phoebe felt as if her shoulder were brushing the rockface. She closed her eyes, held onto the dashboard, and prayed more fervently than she had ever prayed in her life.

But the car behind them was larger and more powerful. It bore down on them like a runaway train, getting nearer and nearer with every twist of the road. Phoebe's heart constricted, and her pulse pounded in her ears. This was it. The crash on the mountain road. Great-Aunt Phoebe's death. It was going to happen all over again.

"There's a wide spot up ahead," Jonathan yelled. "I'm going to pull over and let him pass."

Slowing down was not an option; the car behind them was too close. Jonathan cranked the wheel, whipped the little Roadster onto the shoulder, and braked hard. The Model T shuddered to a stop about three inches from a boulder the size of a small house. The pursuing car roared on by.

"Whew!" Phoebe let out a pent-up breath. "That was close."

"Idiot," Jonathan muttered. "Driving like he's drunk."

"Well, we're safe now." Phoebe leaned over the seat. "You all right back there, Lewis?"

"Sure, I'm great. That was fun—can we do it again?"

"Fun?" Jonathan chuckled. "Sorry, sport—if you thought that was fun, you're going to be extremely bored for the rest of this trip." He pushed the starter button, and the engine sputtered to life. "We'll take it nice and easy from here on out."

Phoebe forced a smile. "You won't get any arguments from me."

"Then let's go. Gatlinburg, here we come!"

◠

Thirty minutes passed, then an hour. Lewis, snuggled up under his blankets in the rumble seat, had fallen asleep. Phoebe felt her own eyelids growing heavy.

"Why don't you take a nap?" Jonathan said. "I'm wide awake, and we've got another hour or so to go."

Phoebe nodded, rested her head on his shoulder, and let sleep overtake her.

◠

She had to be dreaming—a dream born out of the terror of being followed at close range along the dark and dangerous mountain road. She felt the acceleration, sensed the jerk of shifting gears, heard the squeal of tires—she lunged upright, and her eyes snapped open.

It was no dream. Jonathan had both hands gripped tightly on the wheel, and she could see his jaw clenched in an attitude of intense concentration.

"What's wrong?"

But even as she uttered the question, Phoebe knew. Light spilled into the cab of the Roadster from behind. She turned and looked as four huge headlights drew nearer. The engine roared. Closer, closer . . .

WHAM! Metal squealed against metal as the bumpers collided and the Model T lurched forward.

"What does he think he's doing?" Phoebe screamed.

"I believe he was waiting for us. A few minutes back, I passed a big touring car on the side of the road. Packard, Lincoln, Cadillac—something expensive and powerful."

"But who would do this? And why?"

"You know who. And why."

WHAM! The car hit them again, harder this time. Jonathan held on and tried to speed up, swerving the Roadster toward the right.

Then, on a downhill curve, their pursuer swung out into the oncoming lane and accelerated.

"He's going to kill us—or himself!" Phoebe grabbed at Jonathan's arm.

Lewis, now wide awake in the rumble seat, sat up. "What's going on?"

The touring car drew up even with the Roadster, slowing to match their speed. Phoebe turned, intending to shout at the driver, but the words caught in her throat. In a blur, her eyes took in the Cadillac Landau Coupe, the long black hood with its double headlights and sweeping radiator ornament, the wide running boards. A car she had seen before, parked in her own driveway.

"STOP!" she yelled above the rattling of the Model T. "Father, don't!"

He didn't hear, or if he did, he didn't respond. As if in slow motion, she could see his eyes narrowing, his hands tightening around the steering wheel.

"Jonathan, watch out!" she screamed.

The warning came too late. Father wrenched the wheel, scraping the fender of the Landau against the side of the Model T. The Roadster careened and veered sharply to the right.

Phoebe looked up in time to see the side of a cliff of granite hurtling straight toward them. Then she pitched forward, felt a sharp crack against her skull, and descended into cold, black nothingness.

PART 3

Resurrected Dreams

The tomb is dark and safe,
but I cannot lie in wait forever.
If not today, tomorrow
the stone might roll away
to blind me with the dawning light
and chill my wounds
with fresh and healing air.
Death, I am told,
is painful,
but no one speculates what agonies
might come with resurrection.

18

The Third Day

She's waking up."

Phoebe heard the words, muffled and indistinct, like a child's secret whispered through tin cans tied with string. She fought to pry her eyes open, to lift her head, but the effort was too much for her.

"Lie still, honey," the voice said. Then, "Somebody get the doctor."

Her mind followed the sounds: footsteps clicking across a hard floor, a door opening, voices echoing in a hallway, the door shutting again.

She licked her lips and attempted to speak, but her tongue clung to the roof of her mouth. "Water," she croaked.

Someone put a straw to her lips, and with great effort she sucked down the cool liquid. "Thank you," she mumbled.

"You're going to be all right," the voice said. "The doctor's here."

A large, warm hand enveloped hers, and Phoebe tried again to open her eyes, this time with more success. A hazy picture came into focus above her: a gray-haired man with a bulbous nose and a bushy white mustache, dressed in a white coat with something embroidered in red above the pocket—a name. *Barnabas Stowe, M.D.* A stethoscope dangled from his ears. He smiled down at her and lifted her wrist with two huge fingers.

"I'm going to take your pulse and listen to your heart. Just lie still."

Phoebe shut her eyes again and waited, flinching a little when the cold metal disk of the stethoscope touched her skin. "Where . . . where am I?"

"In the hospital," the doctor said. "Took quite a crack in the skull, you did."

Phoebe reached up and touched her fingers to her right temple. She could feel a huge goose egg and several stitches. Her head throbbed miserably.

"I thought I was dead."

"Dead?" The doctor laughed. "You had a bad fall, a nasty concussion, and a split lip. But patients don't usually die from this kind of injury. Not my patients, anyway."

Phoebe frowned, which made her head hurt even worse. A bad fall? What was he talking about? "Car wreck," she corrected. The she remembered and jerked up off the pillow. "What about Jonathan and Lewis? Are they all right?"

"Easy there," the doctor soothed, pushing her gently back down on the bed. "Everything will be fine."

"What is she talking about?" a voice behind Dr. Stowe asked. "Who are Jonathan and Lewis? Is she coherent?"

For the first time, Phoebe became aware of other people in the room, half-hidden in the shadows. A man and several women. It was the man who had spoken.

Stowe held up his hand in front of Phoebe's face, making a *V* with his fingers. "How many?"

"Two," Phoebe answered irritably. "Where are Jonathan and Lewis? Who are all these people?"

Stowe ignored her question. "What's your name?"

"Phoebe Lange," Phoebe answered.

The doctor smiled. "Where do you live? What city?"

"Asheville, North Carolina."

"Very good. And what day is it?"

"Friday," Phoebe said. "No, Saturday. I think."

"It's Sunday," Dr. Stowe said quietly. "You've been unconscious for the past three days. You'll be fine, my dear. Might experience a bit of disorientation for a while, but you'll be good as new in no time." He turned and looked over his shoulder at the visitors. "Five minutes. Then she needs to rest."

In a single motion, the others drew forward and circled around her bed. Phoebe's eyes wouldn't seem to focus, and the effort of moving her head caused shooting pains through her skull. She could vaguely make out the gray-haired lady in a wheelchair, pushed by a large woman dressed in some kind of uniform. There were two other women and one man—all about her age. The walls of the room were a sickly shade of green, the exact color of the way Phoebe felt at this very moment.

The white-haired woman edged to the side of the bed and took Phoebe's hand in hers. "We've been so worried, dear," she said in a whispery voice. "But you're going to be all right now, just as the doctor said."

Phoebe squinted in the old woman's direction. "Gram?"

"Yes, I'm here. We're all here."

"All?"

"Of course. Jake, and your friends. Lovely girls. You should have brought them to visit long before now. Jake called yesterday morning. The three of them came as soon as they heard."

A shadow fell over Phoebe's bed on the other side. She turned her head to see Jake Bartlett smiling down at her. "You gave us quite a scare, sweetheart."

"What . . . what are you doing here?"

"The woman I love is in the hospital with a concussion. Where else would I be?"

"Mildred's here, too—and Ethyle?"

He shook his head. "Still not quite conscious," he muttered. He leaned down over Phoebe. "Krista and Naomi," he said, enunciating carefully. "Remember?"

The two women pressed in close to the bed, one on either

214

side of Jake. "Hey there," Krista said, grinning. "It's good to see you awake."

Naomi brushed her hair out of her eyes. Phoebe could see she had been crying. "I'm so glad you're all right. What would we do without you?"

"Naomi, hush!" Krista hissed, shooting her a withering glare. "It's not like she was dying, you know."

Phoebe tried to smile, but the movement hurt too much. She dropped her head back onto the pillow and shut her eyes. "Thanks for coming," she murmured. She could feel herself drifting, getting further away, sinking back into sleep. "Home. I'm home."

~

The dream was all mixed up—Jake, driving along I-85 between Atlanta and Asheville in a blue Model T Roadster, with Naomi and Krista wedged into the rumble seat. Jonathan standing at her bedside in the hospital, and little Lewis watching her with wide eyes, whispering, "Don't die, Phoebe; please don't die."

When she awoke again, a late-afternoon sun was slanting through the blinds, creating a pattern of dark and light bars across the hospital blanket. In the corner of the room, she could see Jake sprawled in an ugly green-vinyl chair, his long legs stretched out in front of him, his head lolling to one side.

"Jake," she whispered.

"Mmmph," he said and turned his head.

"Jake, wake up." Louder this time.

He stirred and stretched, then opened his eyes. "Sorry. Must have dozed off." He gathered his legs under him and came to the bedside. "How are you feeling?"

"Better. Where's everyone else?"

"Gone home. Your grandmother was exhausted. Nurse Hargraves commanded her to get some rest." He patted her hand. "But don't worry about her. Your gram is doing much better. She'll be well in no time—especially now that she knows you're all right."

"Hargraves." Phoebe made a face.

"She is a piece of work, I'll admit." Jake laughed. "But she's the one who insisted we all stay at the house. She's been wonderful."

"Are we talking about the same woman?"

"You might be surprised to learn that she cares a great deal about you."

Phoebe frowned. "That would surprise me, yes."

"Then you don't read people as well as you read literature. I guess you were surprised to find us here, too—me and Krista and Naomi?"

For a minute Phoebe couldn't speak around the lump in her throat. "I . . . I just—"

"Get used to it," he said. "Get used to the idea that we're going to be here. We all love you." He grinned and touched a gentle finger to the lump on her head. "Even when you're—well, not at your best."

"I must look awful."

"A little like the loser in a schoolyard brawl. But I do like your new haircut. And those bruises are a nice purple color. I think you have a sweater that would match them quite well. But don't worry—you'll get your own beautiful face back very soon. You'll probably have a little scar up there over your eye—it'll give you character."

"I'm not beautiful," she protested, feeling an embarrassed flush creep into her neck. "Never was, never will be."

Jake leaned over her and gazed intently into her eyes. "You're beautiful to me," he said with utmost seriousness. "Always have been, always will be."

Phoebe looked into his face and saw that he meant it. Tears welled in her eyes. "I am so glad you're here," she said.

"So am I," he said. He kissed her once, just briefly, and pulled back. "The doctor says that if you're feeling up to it, you can go home tomorrow morning."

"And what will you do? Go back to Atlanta?"

Jake shook his head. "Not a chance. You're not getting rid of me that easily. I'm sticking close—at least until you're fully recovered."

Phoebe started to argue with him, to tell him it wasn't necessary for him to stay around and baby-sit. But suddenly she realized that she *wanted* him here. Krista and Naomi, too. She had a few things to tell them.

"I'll get the nurse to bring you some supper," Jake was saying as he headed for the door. "And then you can go back to sleep."

"Jake, wait—"

He turned. "What?"

"Will you . . . will you go to Gram's tonight?"

"Do you want me to?"

Phoebe hesitated. "No," she said at last. "I'd really like to have someone here with me. And I'd like it to be you."

He scratched his head as if he were thinking hard about his decision. "Well, I suppose if you twist my arm—" He gazed longingly at the chair in the corner. "That green chair and I have gotten pretty intimate in the past few days. I suppose it would be jealous if I abandoned it now. But there's one little problem."

Phoebe frowned. "What problem?"

"Wouldn't I be compromising your virtue if we spent the night together? We might have to get married right away."

Phoebe felt a warm rush of emotion welling up within her. "I'll take that chance."

Jake pulled the door open and stood silhouetted in the light from the corridor. "I love you, you know." He grinned at her. "Even though you snore."

"I do not snore!"

"Yes, you do. Like a freight train. Like a whole camp of lumberjacks with chain saws. Like—"

"All right, all right." Phoebe laughed. "Go get my dinner, will you? I'm starving."

"Your wish is my command." He bowed grandly and exited the room.

"But I don't snore," she said to the closed door.

A faint, muffled voice came from the other side. "You do. And you always have to have the last word, too."

19

Confession

Monday afternoon found Phoebe lying on the sofa in the library surrounded by Jake, Naomi, and Krista, with Scooter the cat at her feet. A lingering dull headache continued to plague her, although the horrible pounding had subsided. Still, she felt a bit dazed and out of place. She half expected Lewis to barrel into the room without notice, or to look up and see Jonathan Barksdale standing in the doorway.

But it was Jake, not Jonathan, who sat beside her, stroking her hand. It was Jake, not Jonathan, who gazed at her with that expression of love and concern. And it was Krista and Naomi, not Ethyle and Mildred, who hovered around her, urging her to eat soup and crackers and drink gallons of hot tea.

She had come back. Back to reality. Back to the place she belonged.

Yet Phoebe couldn't shake the feeling that the vivid dream she had experienced while she had been unconscious was every bit as real. It had been no ordinary dream, the kind that dribbled out of one's mind like water through open fingers. She could still recall every moment of it as if it had really happened. Could still feel the emotions—the fear when she looked into Father's crazed face, the warmth when she took Jonathan's hand or hugged Lewis, the sense of belonging that came with knowing she was fully known and fully loved.

She wasn't sure she would ever experience those feelings of acceptance again. But she did know it wouldn't be for lack of trying.

All morning, as she had checked out of the hospital, driven home with Jake, and settled herself back in Gram's house, Phoebe had turned over in her mind the options that lay before her. She could go on being the "mystery woman," keeping her secrets to herself, protecting her heart, living in fear of the truth being revealed. Or she could trust the people who loved her, enough to open the gates and let them in.

She had done it once, in her dream. It would be harder in real life, where she had so much to lose. But what might she have to gain?

She was determined to find out.

Phoebe looked up from the sofa to find three pairs of eyes gazing at her. For a moment she said nothing, but simply looked at their dear, familiar faces. Jake, with his tousled blond hair, broad forehead, and guileless blue eyes. He seemed so much more himself in a polo shirt and jeans than he did in his three-piece "lawyer suit." His square, tanned hands caressed her fingers, and the warmth of his touch seeped into her skin.

Naomi had drawn a chair up near the end of the sofa and sat absently arranging and rearranging the afghan over Phoebe's feet, which annoyed Scooter to no end. So serious she was, with dark hair falling over her intense brown eyes, her skin fair and translucent. She had always reminded Phoebe of Snow White—innocent of the power of her own lunar beauty, totally unselfconscious and tuned in to the feelings of others.

Between Naomi and Jake, Krista sat with one leg folded under her and the other moving in time to the beat of some inner music. She was Naomi's opposite—bright, freckled, extroverted, with untamed auburn hair and snapping green eyes. A sun to Naomi's moon, Krista shone with a light all her own. She spoke her mind without bothering to edit her thoughts, smiled readily, laughed freely. New acquaintances often thought her shallow and superficial, but in her own way she was every bit as deep and sensitive as Naomi.

Phoebe swallowed down a lump in her throat, momentarily overcome by a rush of gratitude. These three loved her. Gram loved her. And for the first time, she thought their love just might be sufficient to overcome her fear, the anxiety that still nagged at her.

"I . . . I need to talk to you about something," she said at last. "Something important. Something I haven't known how to say."

A significant glance went around the room, bouncing from Jake to Naomi and back to Krista. No one spoke.

Jake's lips turned up in a little smile. "Are you sure you're ready to do this?"

"I'm sure." Phoebe turned to Naomi. "Could you go into my room and get a couple of things for me? In the drawer of the nightstand, you'll find my journal and an old green book—kind of like a scrapbook, with pictures and stuff in it. And on top of the armoire, a small leather diary. I'd appreciate it if you'd bring those in to me. You can reach the wardrobe using the rocking chair. But be careful."

Naomi got to her feet. "I'll be right back."

When she had left the room, Jake fixed her with a glare. "On top of the armoire? Was that what you were doing when you fell? Hiding something on top of an eight-foot wardrobe?"

"Nine," Phoebe corrected. "It's nine feet high. Don't fuss. I'll explain everything as soon as Naomi gets back."

Naomi returned with the requested items and deposited them in Phoebe's lap. "What's this Memory Book?" she said as she resumed her seat. "It looks really interesting."

"It is," Phoebe answered. "But if you don't mind, we'll get to it later. First, I have something to confess."

She reached into the front pocket of the vinyl-covered notebook and retrieved the newspaper article about her father's release from prison. Then, taking a deep breath, she bit her lip and summoned all her courage.

"I guess you're aware that I haven't quite been myself lately," she began. "I've been preoccupied and kind of withdrawn. Jake, you've tried to get me to talk about what's been bothering me, but I haven't been able to make myself do it." She closed her eyes for a moment. "I've been afraid of what you would think of me."

"What we would *think?*" Krista interrupted. "We're your friends, Phoebe. We love you. There's nothing you could tell us that would make us think less of you. The only way you could possibly drive us away is to do what you've been doing lately— shutting us out." She grinned. "And you see how well that's worked, don't you?"

Naomi elbowed Krista in the ribs. "Could you hush for once, and let her talk?"

Phoebe smiled, then exhaled heavily. "Thanks for the vote of confidence, Krista. But I have to admit that I wasn't sure you'd still stick by me—any of you—once you heard what I had to say. I guess I didn't trust you, didn't trust your love for me. And I'm very sorry for that."

Jake leaned forward. "Go on."

"You all know that Gram raised me after my mother died. Everybody told me it was a terrible accident, and that my father was dead. But it wasn't an accident." She lowered her eyes so she wouldn't have to look at their faces. "My mother was murdered. And my father killed her."

Silence descended over the library, broken only by the sound of Scooter's rumbling purr. Phoebe handed the newspaper clipping to Jake, who scanned it and passed it on around the circle.

"So your father's alive," he said at last. "And he's being released."

Phoebe nodded. "Gram thinks he might want to see me."

Krista let out a little moan. "Oh, Phoeb, what are you going to do? Do you think he might be coming after you? This is awful!"

"What Krista means," Naomi interpreted, "is that we're all very sorry for what you've been going through, and especially that you felt you had to go through it alone." She reached out and patted Phoebe's blanketed foot. "But you don't have to face it by yourself. We're here, and we love you."

"That's right," Jake said, his voice tight. "We're here for you. And if your father does come back, he'll have to go through me to get to you."

Phoebe's mind flashed to that last night with Jonathan, after graduation, how he had put his arms around Lewis and said, *"Your father will have to go through me to get to him."* She stifled tears and forced herself to go on with the rest of the story.

"All my life I've felt . . . well, different. As if something was not quite right. And so I put up a facade—what you call the 'mystery woman,' Jake. I held back, convinced that no one could possibly love me if they knew the real me. I didn't know why— until I saw this newspaper article. Gram kept the real story from me all these years because she wanted me to have a 'normal childhood,' whatever that means. But nothing about my life has been normal. I think I've always known the truth, in the back of my mind, deep down in my soul. I used to have nightmares about it—dreams about my mother dying, about the blood, about a man standing in the shadows."

"And you thought there was something wrong with you because of it," Jake said quietly.

"What else could I think? When Gram told me about the news release, when she told me the truth, she told me something else, too—something that confirmed my worst fears about myself. My father wasn't the first abuser in our family. It's a pattern that has spanned several generations."

"Your grandfather? Gram's husband?" Naomi asked.

"Yes. Lewis." Phoebe's heart wrenched. It was difficult for her to imagine that sweet, loving child growing up into the image of his father. "He abused Gram—not physically, but emotionally. And Lewis's father, my great-grandfather, Gerald, was an alcoholic who beat his only son with a strap." She clenched her teeth and steeled herself against the memory. "Maybe it's in the genes—men who abuse, and women who do nothing to stop it."

"And you were afraid it might happen to you," Jake said. "Afraid of me. That's why you pulled back and became so distant. Have I ever touched you except in love? Have I ever bullied you or tried to control you? Ever shown any indication—any sign at all . . ." He stammered into silence, unable to go on.

Tears pooled in his eyes, and his gentle face contorted in a mask of pain. "You have *never* hurt me, Jake," Phoebe answered. "You have only shown me love and respect. I know it doesn't make sense, but try to understand. I had to come to some comprehension of the pattern and some resolution with the past, if I was ever going to trust my own instincts and get beyond my fear."

"Even if there were some catalyst that pushed your family down this path," Krista put in, "what difference would it make? You might be able to stop the pattern now, in the present, but you can't change the past."

The response that came to Phoebe's mind was, *I know. I tried, and it didn't work.* But she didn't say that. Instead she simply sighed and said, "Right. You can't change the past."

"And you can't possibly know what set off the pattern in the first place, either," Naomi added. "Some terrible tragedy, some incurable wound? Alcoholism? That sort of thing often goes back for generations. Most likely all those people are long dead. Who do you ask to find an answer?"

For a minute or two Phoebe didn't respond. She sat there, running her hands over the cover of her great-aunt's Memory Book. "You go to the source," she said at last. "Or at least the closest source you can find."

She held up the Memory Book, with its bowed green cover and faded lettering. "Meet the woman who shares my name," she said. "My great-aunt, Phoebe Elizabeth Lange. Born 1909, died 1927. This is her Memory Book, and this"—she pointed to the small leather journal in her lap—"this is her diary. Great-Aunt Phoebe has helped me find some of my answers."

Phoebe lifted her gaze, looked around at them. She had half expected disbelief or incredulity or even skepticism. Instead she saw in their eyes a willingness to hear what she had to say, a receptiveness that bolstered her courage and enabled her to go on.

This time she wouldn't hold back. She would tell them everything—the Memory Book, the journal entries, her strange and vivid dream. All of it. Whether they believed her or not, she would take the risk.

20

A Very Odd Story

Phoebe watched the three of them around the circle as Great-Aunt Phoebe's Memory Book passed from hand to hand. Each face registered a variety of emotions—curiosity, intrigue, astonishment—but all their expressions reflected interest.

"So, what do you think?" she said.

Naomi shut the book, laid it on the edge of the sofa, and fixed Phoebe with an intense gaze. "I for one think it's fascinating. All these photos and personal memorabilia and notes from friends. It's like a slice of living history. But I'm more interested in hearing *your* reaction."

Both Jake and Krista nodded, encouraging Phoebe to go on with the tale.

"When, thanks to Scooter, I discovered the Memory Book," Phoebe said, "my initial response was absolute amazement that there was another Phoebe Lange who had lived nearly seventy-five years ago. I felt as if I had stepped back in time, into someone else's

231

skin. It was all very intriguing. But then I found out something else about this other Phoebe Lange, something that convinced me she might have more to offer me than just an interesting diversion, a trip down memory lane. That she might hold some answers to my questions about my father—and my heritage." She paused and took a deep breath. "Phoebe Lange was my great-aunt. My grandfather's sister."

Krista furrowed her brow in a frown. "So?"

"So," Naomi explained, "Phoebe—the old Phoebe—was Lewis's sister. Lewis was our Phoebe's father's father."

Krista looked more confused than ever. "Huh?"

Jake grinned. "Let me try." He turned to Krista. "What Naomi is trying to say is that the woman who compiled this Memory Book wasn't just some shirttail relative. She was Lewis Lange's older sister. Lewis bullied Gram, and probably Phoebe's father, too, setting in motion the pattern of abuse. So if Phoebe could find out more about the older Phoebe's life, she might be able to understand more about why her father became violent with her mother. Does that help?"

Krista's expression softened. "A little. I think."

Jake shifted his attention back to Phoebe. "Go on, please."

"All right. But let me back up a bit." Phoebe paused for a moment, sorting out her thoughts. "When I read through the Memory Book, I was overwhelmed by the parallels between Great-Aunt Phoebe's life and my own. There's an astonishing physical resemblance between us, and other similarities as well. Take her two best friends, Ethyle and Mildred, for example. Ethyle was an extrovert, an adventurer like you, Krista. Mildred was stable and serious and kept Phoebe balanced, like you do for me, Naomi. Jonathan Barksdale—" Phoebe stopped suddenly as she felt a flush of embarrassment creep up her neck. "Well, Jonathan loved her completely. He was a considerate, sensitive, good man. A caring, selfless man. And he even has the same initials as you, Jake."

"Hmm. So he does." Jake smiled.

"Anyway, I began to get this idea that Great-Aunt Phoebe could answer some of my questions, if I could only find a way to get into her mind. Gram told me that Grandpa Lewis had suffered a great deal of grief and loss in his childhood. His mother died giving birth to him. His sister—that's Great-Aunt Phoebe—raised him, but then she died, too, when Lewis was only six. Gram knew some of this from other sources, relatives who told her the story. Grandpa Lewis, she said, was very closemouthed about the whole situation. He never talked about his father at all, and rarely spoke Phoebe's name."

"Then how did you know that Lewis's father was an alcoholic who beat his son?" Naomi asked. "Or all those details about Phoebe's friends?"

Phoebe hesitated, her heart sinking. She had painted herself into a corner and hadn't the faintest idea how she was going to escape. There was no way on earth to explain this without all of them thinking she had lost her mind. But she had to try.

"I'll get to that. In talking with Gram, I learned that Great-Aunt Phoebe had also kept a diary of sorts—a journal." She held up the small brown leather book. "It had been lost, hidden away for a very long time—probably since before her death. Even Lewis hadn't succeeded in finding it."

"But *you* found it," Krista interrupted. "How?"

Phoebe's stomach twisted into a knot. "That's a little hard to explain. It has to do with the parallels I sensed between me and Great-Aunt Phoebe. We seemed so much alike." She stopped short. If she told them about the dream, about seeing Great-Aunt Phoebe on the mountaintop and hearing her voice, they really would think she was nuts.

Jake saved her. "So you reasoned that her hiding place for the journal might be the same secret place you had as a young girl."

Phoebe stared at him. "How did you know I had a secret hiding place?"

He shrugged. "Don't all girls have secret places?"

"I didn't," Krista said.

"You've never had a secret of any kind—or an unexpressed thought," Naomi jibed. "Now, let her get on with the story."

"Jake is right," Phoebe continued. "When I was a child—at least when I became old enough not to be afraid of the tower room—I used to hide in the armoire. It was my special place. Since Great-Aunt Phoebe had occupied the same room, I thought she might be partial to the wardrobe, too. I found the diary hidden on the top, behind the decorative molding."

"Then you fell off the rocking chair trying to get it down," Krista supplied, "and ended up with a cracked skull, seven stitches, a concussion, and three nights in the hospital."

"No, she couldn't have fallen trying to get the diary *down* from its hiding place," Naomi countered with unshakable logic. "Or else she wouldn't know what she knows about Lewis Lange. Great-Aunt Phoebe must have written about him in the diary, and Phoebe read it."

Phoebe's mind raced. Here was her out. She could claim to have read the diary from cover to cover, and learned from it everything she knew about Lewis and about Great-Aunt Phoebe's life. But that wouldn't be honest. Besides, she had already promised herself that she would be completely candid with her friends, and leave the outcome to a wiser judge. Going back on that vow would be a violation of her own integrity.

She took a deep breath. "Actually, the truth lies somewhere in between. I did read part of Great-Aunt Phoebe's journal—the first few entries, anyway. But then Hargraves interrupted me, and I went to put it back in its place on top of the wardrobe. That's when I fell and hit my head."

"Do you mean to tell us that you *haven't* read it?" Jake said.

"Not all of it. Only a few entries."

Naomi leaned forward. "Then where did you come by all this information about Phoebe and Lewis and her friends and this love of her life—what's his name?"

"Jonathan. Jonathan Barksdale."

"You're holding something back," Krista said. "I can see it in your eyes. Come on, give."

"You'll all think I'm crazy."

"We think you're crazy now." Krista grinned.

When Phoebe didn't laugh, Naomi jumped in. "She didn't mean that, Phoebe. You're the sanest person we know. But we are interested in hearing what you have to say."

What Phoebe wanted most at this moment was to run, to hide, to climb into the wardrobe and shut the door until all three of them had given up and gone back to Atlanta. It would be so much easier just to keep everything to herself, to live without the pain that vulnerability brought. But that would also mean living without love, without friendship. Safe, but alone.

She closed her eyes, and a series of images surfaced in her mind. The dream—it seemed years ago now—in which she witnessed the crucifixion of the little boy. That morning sitting around the kitchen table with Jonathan and Ethyle and Mildred, the day she told them about Father's abuse of Lewis and her own shame and fear. Her confession to her friends—or rather, Great-Aunt Phoebe's friends—that she felt as if God had abandoned her. And Jonathan's empathetic response: *"God has not abandoned you. We're here."*

In the role of Great-Aunt Phoebe, she had prayed, and God—or someone—had responded. She had been embraced with love and acceptance. Her burdens had been lightened by the strong and willing arms of those around her. Her fears had been allayed, and her courage fortified.

But that was in a dream. Would it work here, in the real world, with real people capable of rejecting her?

Phoebe didn't know. But the decision had already been made. From somewhere deep in her soul, the prayer formed of its own accord: *God, give me wisdom. Give me strength. Give me courage. Give me faith.*

She opened her eyes. They were waiting, watching her with unguarded curiosity.

It was time to tell the weirdest part of this very odd story.

21

The Dream

I remember falling and hitting my head," Phoebe said cautiously. "Then it seemed as if I woke up somewhere else."

Naomi tilted her head. "You did. You woke up in the hospital, three days later."

"That's not what I mean, exactly. It was more like I woke up in some other time. I was still in the tower bedroom, but Lewis was there, as a little boy. And Father—Lewis's father, Gerald Lange. And Jonathan."

"Jonathan Barksdale, Great-Aunt Phoebe's beau," Krista supplied.

"Yes. It was as if I had been thrust back in time, to 1927, and was playing the role of Great-Aunt Phoebe at age eighteen."

For a minute or two no one said a word. Then a light came on in Krista's face. "A dream! You were having a dream, while you were unconscious after the concussion."

"It must have been a dream," Phoebe agreed. "I have no other explanation. But it was the most vivid, realistic dream I've ever experienced. I was there, back in 1927, for a week. I met Lewis—a loving, tender, vulnerable little boy. I witnessed the results of Father's beatings, saw how violent the man could be when he was drunk. The pattern did not start with Lewis. He was a victim of it."

Naomi frowned. "But that's no excuse. He's still responsible for what he did to your grandmother—and for the way he raised your father."

"Yes, he is. It's not an excuse. But it is a reason."

"And Jonathan?" Jake asked. "What about Jonathan?"

"Ooh," Krista said, "do I detect a note of jealousy?"

Jake's face flushed red. "I'm not jealous. I just want to know what happened, what kind of insights Phoebe got from this—this dream."

"Lewis adored Jonathan, and the feeling was obviously mutual," Phoebe continued. "I suppose Jonathan was the only man Lewis knew who treated him as a person, not as a punching bag. And I—that is, Great-Aunt Phoebe—was furious with Father for the way he treated her brother. But she was afraid of him, too.

"I suppose, in a way, Father was also a victim—not of someone else's abuse, as far as I know, but of his own pain and grief. He never got over losing his wife, and illogical as it might seem, he blamed Lewis for her death. The alcohol removed any modicum of self-control he might have otherwise exercised."

"So the pattern goes back for generations," Naomi said.

"That still doesn't justify what they did—your grandfather, his father, all of them."

"No, it doesn't." Phoebe shook her head. "When I first read that newspaper article and found out my father had murdered my mother, I didn't care what extenuating circumstances were involved. I hated him, hated my grandfather, too. But then I . . . well, I found out what Lewis's father had done to him. He was such a wonderful little boy and—" She stammered to a halt, biting back tears.

"And you saw all this in . . . in your dream?" Jake asked.

Phoebe nodded. "It was so real. It was as if I were actually there. Seeing the bruises on Lewis's arms and legs. Hearing him being beaten through the closed door of Father's study." She took a deep breath, steadied herself, and went on: "I felt Great-Aunt Phoebe's fear. And then I . . . I did something. Something I'm not sure Great-Aunt Phoebe did back in 1927."

Krista and Naomi leaned forward. "What?" they said in unison.

"I agreed to marry Jonathan Barksdale." Her eyes cut to Jake's face. "As Great-Aunt Phoebe, of course."

Jake said nothing.

"As far as I could tell—both from what little I read in the journal and what I experienced in the dream, Great-Aunt Phoebe had never told a soul about her father's drinking or his abuse of Lewis. But I did. It took every bit of courage I could muster, but I told Jonathan and Ethyle and Mildred everything that was happening.

And together we formulated a plan. Right after graduation, Jonathan and I would elope, run away to Gatlinburg and get married. Ethyle and Mildred would look after Lewis until we got back, and then Lewis would come to live with me and Jonathan, where he could be protected.

"Only Father got wind of the fact that Jonathan and I were planning to elope. He was furious, and he would have beaten Lewis nearly to death if I hadn't intervened. Then he attacked me, too." She touched her lip. The split was healing, but it was still raw and tender.

"I don't know what I was thinking. It was a crazy idea, but I actually believed that I might be able to change what happened to Lewis—and ultimately, to my father and my mother."

Krista lifted one eyebrow and grinned. "Haven't you seen enough episodes of *Star Trek* to convince you not to go messing with the space/time continuum?"

Phoebe laughed, and some of the tension in her body drained away. "I should know better, shouldn't I? But at the time—in the dream—it seemed vitally important to try. I couldn't just sit by and do nothing."

"And so you agreed to marry Jonathan Barksdale." Jake's voice was low, subdued.

"Oh, for heaven's sake, Jake," Naomi sputtered. "It's not like she was being unfaithful to you! It was just a dream."

Phoebe felt a little twist in her gut. Yes. It was a dream. It had to have been a dream. And yet she remembered all too

242

acutely the feelings she had had for Jonathan. She couldn't blame Jake too much for being uncomfortable with the idea of her marrying someone else.

"We were planning to leave for Gatlinburg on Saturday morning, the day after graduation," she continued. "Father had been arrested for the assault on me and Jonathan, and wasn't supposed to be arraigned until Monday morning. But he showed up at commencement, during my valedictory address—"

"You were *valedictorian?*" Naomi interrupted.

"Great-Aunt Phoebe was valedictorian," Phoebe corrected. "I read her speech. Anyway, when Father appeared, we didn't know if he had broken out of jail or what he might do, so we decided to leave town right then, late on Friday night. Jonathan and I took Lewis, got in the car, and started north toward Tennessee."

"But you never got there," Jake guessed. "That's why the Memory Book ends with the graduation announcement."

"No. We never got there." Phoebe shook her head. "Father followed us—we didn't know it was him at first—and tried to run us off the road. We got away from him once, but he returned, and rammed us, and sent us flying into the sheer face of the mountain. I hurtled forward, went through the windshield, I guess. Then I woke up. In the hospital, with all of you around me."

No one said anything. Jake bit his lip. Naomi fiddled with the afghan that covered Phoebe's legs. Krista shifted in her chair.

"You do believe me?"

"Yes," Jake said at last. "Of course. It must have been an

extremely powerful dream, for you to recall it in so much detail. But I'm not certain it's a very reliable source of information. It seems to me more likely that your own life experiences got translated into the dream-world."

"Sure," Naomi said, her brow knit with concentration. "It's all there—two best friends, a sensational fiancé, a terrible secret about your father, all mixed with your frustration about not being able to do anything to change what happened."

Phoebe sat quietly, her heart sinking, while they analyzed the dream. Everything they said made sense, of course, and put the fragmented pieces into a logical sort of order. But she couldn't help feeling as if some of the wonder of the experience was being pulled apart, one thread at a time.

"Or there's another possibility," Jake said when the conversation lulled.

Phoebe snapped to attention. "What's that?"

"That it really happened," Krista put in with an impish grin. "That you really were there, back in 1927."

Jake shook his head. "Not exactly what I had in mind. I was about to say that maybe this dream has *more* significance than we're giving it, not less." He turned to Phoebe and took her hand in his. "You wanted to do something, to put a halt to the pattern of violence you had discovered. Of course, the past couldn't be altered, but perhaps something else did change."

Phoebe gazed at him. "Me, you mean?" she said quietly. "Maybe I'm different?"

"Tell me," he entreated. "How are you different?"

Phoebe thought for a moment. "In the dream, in the role of Great-Aunt Phoebe, I took the risk to tell my friends the truth about my father. Then when I woke up here, with all of you, I found the courage to risk telling you what I didn't want you to know."

Naomi nodded. "About your own father. About what he did to your mother."

"But I'm still afraid," Phoebe said, tears clogging her throat. "Afraid of what might happen if he comes back here. Afraid of what all of you will think of me. Afraid of having to face this alone."

Jake slid out of his chair and perched on the edge of the sofa, drawing Phoebe into a fierce embrace. "You're not alone," he whispered. "We're here. And whatever you have to face, we'll face it together."

It was exactly the right thing to say, precisely the words Phoebe was hoping to hear. The sentiment should have assured her. She waited, hoping against hope for that sense of liberation she had felt with Jonathan, Ethyle, and Mildred. That feeling of being set free to be herself, without worrying what other people thought of her.

She waited.

But it never came.

22

Alone Again

Finally, they had all gone away.

Not permanently, but at least for a little while. After pestering her for half an hour, trying to get her to agree to go to a matinee and dinner, Jake had finally given in to Phoebe's insistence and left the house with Krista and Naomi in tow.

Now Phoebe leaned back in the leather library chair and breathed a sigh of relief. Her pardon would be short-lived, she knew. Two hours, maybe three. Blessed little solitude for an introvert like her, but she intended to make the most of it.

They meant well, she was certain. But for the past few days the three of them had fluttered around her like moths at a gas lamp, fluffing her pillows, covering her feet, bringing her enough soup and tea to float a battleship. Krista talked constantly, making jokes to try to get Phoebe to laugh. Naomi hovered, anticipating what she needed before she even asked. Jake showed her so much consideration that Phoebe feared she might smother under the weight of his attentiveness.

They were trying hard to demonstrate their love and support. Why, then, did Phoebe feel so utterly alone?

She had done the right thing, she believed, in telling them about her father, and about what she had learned of her family from Great-Aunt Phoebe's Memory Book and diary. But something was wrong. She didn't have that sense of freedom and release she had experienced in the dream-world, when she had first opened up to Jonathan and Mildred and Ethyle. It had never come. She just felt more vulnerable than ever, and more insecure.

In addition, she found herself missing the people she had grown to love in Great-Aunt Phoebe's world. Lewis and Jonathan, Ethyle and Mildred. Even, she might say, herself. She knew it hadn't been real, those few days she spent in her great-aunt's skin, and yet Phoebe couldn't shake the feeling that she was more herself in 1927 than she had ever been in the twenty-first century.

She didn't know why. She might never find the answer to that particular question. But for the time being, while on reprieve from the overwhelming presence of Jake and Krista and Naomi, she would spend a few hours in the past, and try to find herself again.

Phoebe looked out the window. The sky had gone gray, and rain was threatening. She flipped on the lamp beside the chair, opened Great-Aunt Phoebe's diary, and began to read.

Friday, May 6, 1927

Phoebe paused. May 6—the opening day of the dream, the first day she stepped into Great-Aunt Phoebe's role. Exactly a week before graduation, before leaving to elope, before the car crash on the road to Gatlinburg. Only a few days before she had blown the whistle on Father, before she had agreed to marry Jonathan. She remembered, in the dream, seeing the date in the diary, but nothing had been written after that. Now there was a long entry, which she read eagerly.

Why am I so fearful of talking with Jonathan and Ethyle and Mildred about all that is going on in this house? Or even Mrs. Bellwether at school, who has been so nice to me and so encouraging about my plans for the future? And why, though I pray and pray, do I still not sense the presence of God, or God's willingness to hear and answer me?

Everyone sees me as the girl who has it all. I have wonderful friends and a beau who (I think) loves me. I have a bright future ahead of me, or so people like Mrs. Bellwether keep saying. And yet privately, in the depths of my heart, I feel empty, unfulfilled. Closed tight, like a mummy in a sarcophagus, surrounded by unimaginable wealth, but devoid of life.

And so I ask myself the question that has been plaguing me: how can I be filled with life again? How can the tomb be opened when there is so much darkness and death inside?

A voice in the back of my mind keeps saying, "Return to Me. Return to yourself." The voice of God's Spirit, perhaps?

I once loved God and believed that God was, indeed, the Immanuel, God with us. But if loving people and being open with them makes you vulnerable to hurt, how much more can you be hurt by opening yourself to the most powerful force in the universe? If death is painful, how much more agonizing might resurrection be?

Still, I know in the deepest part of my heart that I can never be filled unless I am willing to be open. And openness means not just telling the truth, saying the words I am afraid to say, but offering my soul on an altar, knowing I might be hurt in far worse ways than I have ever known. My heart quails at the prospect. The risk is so great. And yet I am approaching the point of no return, the point at which any risk is worth taking.

I have been writing, in my valedictory address, about such risk, about giving up everything for the Pearl of Great Price. But is my own soul prepared to be open for business, ready to be honest with God and with others, willing to negotiate for the Pearl of Great Price?

I have just reread the previous sentence and am overcome by an awareness of my own foolishness. There is no negotiating for that Pearl. It will cost everything I have, everything I am, everything I ever will be—present, past, and future. And yet I have to cling to the hope that the prize will be worth the price.

Still, even if I am willing to risk it all, how do I set about doing that? What does God want from me? In the midst of my current confusion, only one thing comes to mind, a principle I learned years ago: "What does the Lord require of you but to do justice, love mercy, and walk humbly with your God?"

Some childhood Sunday school teacher made me memorize that verse, and now it will not let go of me. But perhaps it holds my answer. Active justice for Lewis, merciful love in my relationship with Jonathan, humility and intimacy in my connection with God.

Perhaps I do not need to map out the whole path. Perhaps all I need to do is take the one known step that lies before me now and leave the rest of the unknowns to Someone who sees the way more clearly than I.

I could be hurt, in both body and soul. I could be rejected and left alone. But I will never know unless I try.

Justice for Lewis. Love for Jonathan.

And perhaps, God willing, freedom for me.

Phoebe closed the book and smiled. She had done it. Great-Aunt Phoebe had set aside her fears, opened herself to being hurt, trusted God and the people she loved. A remembered rush of elation surged into Phoebe's heart. Then, like a balloon losing air, Phoebe exhaled that feeling of exhilaration on a whooshing sigh. She sank back into the chair cushion, totally deflated. What difference did it make how real the dream seemed? It was still just a dream.

It doesn't matter whether it was a dream or not, a voice in the back of her mind whispered.

Phoebe tensed for an internal argument. Of course it mattered. Sane people knew the difference between fact and fantasy. Sane people lived in the present, not in the past. Sane people kept a firm hold on what was real.

The truth is real, the voice said.

Phoebe thought about that for a minute. She had spent the last five years of her life immersing herself in the great literature of the Western world. None of it was, strictly speaking, *real*. It was all the product of imagination. And yet Milton and Shakespeare and Spenser and Donne communicated truth in their poems and stories and dramas. Human truth. Spiritual truth. A truth much more profound than most of what went on in the mundane lives of people in the so-called "real world."

In that sense, at least, the voice of her alter ego was right. Truth was real; reality was not always true.

But what was the truth she could hold to from this dream-world she had experienced? She had followed Great-Aunt

Phoebe's example and opened herself up to her friends. She had revealed the hidden secret. And yet she still felt alone, still afraid.

There is no fear in love, the voice murmured in her ear. *Perfect love casts out fear.*

The answer blinked on in Phoebe's mind, a bright flash, as if someone had flipped a switch. She had revealed her *secrets.* She had not revealed *herself.* Not really. She was still holding back, still protecting herself. She had not given all for the Pearl of Great Price. She was still afraid, and as long as she held onto the fear, she could not reach out and receive the love.

But what was she so afraid of?

The words of Great-Aunt Phoebe's journal returned to her: *If loving people and being open with them makes you vulnerable to hurt, how much more can you be hurt by opening yourself to the most powerful force in the universe? If death is painful, how much more agonizing might resurrection be?*

She was afraid to be open with God.

It didn't make sense—at least not on the surface. God was love. The Bible said so, and other people certainly seemed to believe it. If that was true, then being vulnerable to God ought to be the safest move in the world.

But it didn't feel safe. Not in a world that offered so much tragedy and so little justice. A world where mommies could die and daddies could kill them without God lifting a finger to intervene.

Phoebe felt herself shrinking, shrinking, until she was back there again, at age five, creeping into the living room to see what all the noise was about. Mama lying on the floor with blood pouring from her head. A man standing over Mama, with something in his hand. His head turning, fixing that icy gaze on her, those pale blue eyes—

She shook her head, forcing herself back to the present. Still full of rage and pain and fear aroused by the terrible memory, she lifted her fist toward the ceiling.

"God," she muttered through clenched teeth, "I'm not sure I trust you enough to open myself to you. I can accept the premise that you didn't do this to my mother, but I also know that you didn't stop it from happening, either. I've been mad at you—really mad. And yet I don't want to go on this way, keeping my soul to myself and never experiencing the freedom I knew in that dream. So if you're listening, God, this is your chance to show me what you're made of. It's the only invitation you'll get."

Then, spent and exhausted, Phoebe laid her head back on the chair and stared out the window at the drizzly gray afternoon.

23

The Prodigal Father

The dream came again. As always, Phoebe saw her mother fall, saw the blood, saw the man standing over her with something in his hand. She stood frozen with terror, unable to move, unable to scream, unable to help. He turned his gaze on her—those ice-blue eyes that chilled her straight through to her soul.

But this time the dream was different.

For one thing, she wasn't the five-year-old Phoebe, a little girl cowering in fear as her mommy died. She was her adult self, watching with a more critical eye. The man seemed clearer, more defined. Bigger than she remembered.

But how could he have been bigger? If she was older, then logic dictated he ought to have seemed smaller by comparison. And yet there he was, a huge hulking form in the darkness, towering over her, staring down at her.

And something else was different, too.

She was not alone.

She couldn't see them, but she could feel them, a palpable presence. Three of them. Jake, Krista, and Naomi. Or maybe it was Jonathan, Ethyle, and Mildred. She couldn't tell. She could only sense them standing off to one side in the shadows, reaching out to her. She could feel their nearness radiating warmth and strength into her.

She understood. They couldn't change what had happened, any more than she could. But they were there. They loved her.

Then she heard a sound behind her, coming not from her three friends, but from someone else. A fourth person, someone she couldn't see or identify. An unusual sort of voice—deep and resonant, but not exactly male; lilting and gentle, but not exactly female. The voice was crying, and the sound reminded Phoebe of the tolling of bells, the beating of wings, the singing of stars. A cosmic mourning, as if all heaven and earth were weeping for her loss.

In the dream, she turned and looked behind her. There was nothing there. Yet the weeping continued, and out of the corner of her eye she caught the smallest glimmer of movement, a momentary distortion of light, like the shifting of a prism.

~

Phoebe awoke with a jolt. Her pillow was damp with tears, and someone was shaking her. She opened her eyes and squinted against the sunlight pouring in through the tower window.

"Phoebe, wake up."

"I'm awake." She struggled to a sitting position and tried to focus. It was Naomi, fully dressed and looking seriously disturbed. "What time is it?" Phoebe asked.

"Nine-thirty." Naomi sat down on the side of the bed. "You need to get up. Something's happened."

"Gram? Is she all right?" Phoebe tried to get out of bed, but Naomi put a hand on her shoulder. "Your grandmother's fine. Much better; nearly back to her old self." Naomi bit her lip.

"Then, what's all the fuss about? From the look on your face, you'd think somebody died."

"Nobody died. It's just that—well, he's here."

"Who's here?"

"Your father. He wants to see you."

Phoebe felt all the blood drain from her head, and a chill ran through her. She pulled the comforter up around her shoulders. "You're joking."

"I'm afraid not."

"He thinks he can just waltz in here and demand to see me, just like that?"

"Apparently so. Jake and your grandmother are with him now, in the study. We told him you had just been released from the hospital, and that you weren't really up to seeing anyone, but he was very insistent. Said he had to explain things to you."

A white-hot anger rose up in Phoebe's gut. She could still see the vivid images from the dream—her mother limp as a rag doll on the floor, her father standing over his victim with a tire iron.

"What's there to explain?" Phoebe said. "He killed my

mother and served twenty years of a life sentence. Now he expects to come back, having paid his debt to society, so to speak, and take up with his long-lost daughter like nothing ever happened?"

Naomi recoiled from the rage. "You want us to get rid of him?"

Phoebe stared at her, trying to decide what to do. She might never have another chance to confront him, to tell the man what she thought of him. She lifted her eyes to Naomi's. "No. Tell him I'll be down as soon as I've had a shower. He's going to have to look me in the eye and see how much damage he's done."

Naomi nodded, patted Phoebe's hand, and got up to leave.

"Wait," Phoebe said. "What's he like?"

"He's an old man." Naomi shrugged. "A sick, tired, broken old man."

The study door was closed. Behind it, Phoebe could hear the low murmur of voices. She stood there for a minute, summoning her nerve, all the while recalling other voices heard through this very same door. Lewis begging Father not to beat him. Father yelling. The sound of the strap as it cut into Lewis's tender flesh.

She closed her eyes, took a deep breath, and turned the knob.

Jake and Gram sat in two armchairs at right angles to the fireplace. In a third chair sat an emaciated, wizened little man. He rose shakily to his feet when she entered.

Phoebe's eyes swept over him. He was wearing khaki pants and a matching long-sleeved shirt, the kind of work gear worn by manual laborers. The clothes, so new that they still had creases in them from the packaging, hung on his thin frame like rags on a scarecrow. His eyes were sunk back in his skull, and three days' growth of gray beard stubbled his chin and neck. He was not yet sixty, and yet he looked older than Gram. If she had seen him on the street, she most likely would have directed him to the nearest homeless shelter.

He approached her cautiously and held out a gnarled and horny hand. Phoebe pulled back.

Gram got up, came over to her, and put a protective arm around Phoebe's shoulders. "Phoebe, you may not remember, but this is your father, Jude Lange." Her voice was cold, distant.

"H-hello," Phoebe stammered. All her resolve to blast this man to kingdom come had vanished the instant she laid eyes on him. He carried himself like a refugee, a survivor of Auschwitz or Dachau. Head down, shoulders hunched, eyes fixed on the ground. This was not what she had anticipated, not at all.

"I'm glad to see you, Phoebe," he said in a voice cracked with disuse. "I've thought about you every day for the past twenty years."

Mute with disbelief, Phoebe stared at him. What did he expect? That she would run into his arms and weep on his shoulder? That she would call out the musicians and kill the fatted calf to celebrate his return? That this would turn out to be a happy reunion of father and daughter, so long separated and at last brought together again?

Phoebe didn't even know this man. But she did know what he had done. His act of violence had haunted her since she was five years old. He had taken her mother from her, left her as an orphan. He had violated her trust, undermined the fundamental bond between parent and child.

Yes, she had only been five. But she still remembered—a memory reinforced by the dream that came to her over and over again.

She closed her eyes and could still see the images burned upon her brain: the large, hulking form standing over her dying mother. That icy blue gaze, devoid of conscience or compassion—

Phoebe's eyes snapped open. He was still standing there, waiting, his hand outstretched. He was half a head shorter than Phoebe. So small, so frail, his shoulders hunched and rounded by the burden he had borne for the past twenty years. He could have lost weight, but he couldn't have lost that much height.

And his eyes—

Phoebe felt the bottom drop out of her stomach.

His eyes were brown.

24

Jude's Tale

Phoebe stared at him. He stared back.

Out of the corner of her eye she saw Krista and Naomi enter, hovering in the doorway. Silence filled the room, and a roaring like distant surf pounded in her ears. Her legs wouldn't hold her.

Jake got up and steered her to the chair he had vacated. She sank into it, her whole body trembling. Her eyes never left the face of the old man as he, too, resumed his seat.

No one spoke. To Phoebe, it seemed as if the entire universe were holding its breath, waiting. Waiting for her to make a move.

She cleared her throat and tried to find her voice. For a moment or two she sat mute, as she had been so many times in her nightmare—trying to scream, but unable to produce a sound. And when her voice finally came, it formed words she never dreamed she'd utter.

"You didn't do it."

She felt Jake's hand clamp down on her shoulder, heard a sharp intake of breath from the doorway, saw Gram's hand jerk upward to her mouth. All these sensations came to her brain in a haze, as if the room were filled with fog. Only from Jude Lange's craggy countenance did an unseen breeze push the mist away; his face was as clear in her view as if etched in stone.

One tear leaked out from his right eye and traced its way, unchecked, down the seams of his stubbled face.

"You didn't do it," she repeated. "You didn't kill my mother."

He focused his eyes on his stiff new shoes and shook his head. "No." A shaky hand tried to scrub the tear away, but it was no use. More tears came, and his bony shoulders shook with the sobbing.

Jake knelt beside her chair. "Are you sure, Phoebe?"

She didn't look at him. She kept her eyes fixed on Jude Lange. Her father. "I'm sure. I remember. The man who killed my mother was a big man, tall and hulking. And his eyes were blue."

Jude lifted his head and looked into Phoebe's face. He was so old, so completely broken, a fragile shell of the man he must have been in his youth. And yet she could still see in those bloodshot eyes a shadow of what she had seen in the mirror every day of her life.

She had his eyes.

Brown eyes.

Innocent eyes.

~

Half an hour later, the six of them were gathered around the breakfast table. Jude ate like a man starved—three servings of scrambled eggs, four slices of toast, half a dozen strips of bacon. Gram sat next to him, patting his arm, gazing at him and blinking back tears. Her only son, raised from the dead and restored to her.

Phoebe waited, a little impatiently, until he had finished his breakfast and pushed his plate back from the edge of the table. She refilled his coffee cup, resumed her seat, and looked at him. "Do we get the whole story now?"

Jude nodded and took a deep breath. "I loved your mother," he said quietly. "I really did. And I loved you." He shook his head sadly. "The problem was, I loved the bottle more. When you were about three, I came home drunk and lashed out. I didn't mean to, but it was the last straw for Marie. She had me arrested, left me, and brought you here to stay with Mom.

"The reality of losing her—and you—was the jolt I needed to get sober. I was out of jail in three months, but I knew I couldn't come back until I had licked the drinking. It took nearly a year and a half, but I finally did it. Got clean, got a job, knew I could make it. I came back, and she gave me another chance." He clenched his jaw. "Then the unthinkable happened."

Phoebe leaned forward. She didn't want to hear this, and yet she did. She had to know, once and for all. "What happened the night she was killed?" Phoebe whispered.

He exhaled heavily. "We had just moved into a new apartment. Money was tight. Your mother still didn't quite trust me, and as it turned out, she was right. I was feeling . . . well, a little trapped. We had an argument. I left in a huff and went on a binge."

Jake raised an eyebrow. "You fell off the wagon?"

"Yeah. Big time. Found a little bar, blew most of the week's wages. I was drunk—really drunk. Somehow I managed to drive home, and when I got there, the place was crawling with police cars and ambulances. A crowd had gathered, and someone told me a woman had been killed. I knew in my gut it was Marie. I panicked and ran."

"And left your five-year-old daughter to fend for herself?" Naomi frowned.

"Believe me, I'm not proud of what I did," he said tightly. "But I was scared. I had been in jail before, once when I had lost control and hit Marie. I never did it again, but that record followed me. Alcohol does strange things to a man's logic. I knew Mom would be there for you, Phoebe, and I figured you'd be better off with her."

"OK," Jake said. "You were scared, and you ran. But why didn't you leave town?"

"I couldn't—not until I knew for sure that Phoebe was all right." He shook his head. "I laid low for a couple of days. But then after the funeral—"

"You were there," Phoebe interrupted. "At the grave site. Standing in the rain."

"You saw me?"

"I didn't recognize you. But I saw a man, off in the distance, watching. You disappeared before I could get Gram to look."

He nodded. "I had to say good-bye. Then I went and drank myself into oblivion."

"And the police caught up with you in the bar that night," Jake said.

"That's right." Jude ran a hand over his face. "They arrested me for the murder."

Naomi leaned forward and asked the question that was on everyone's mind. "If you didn't kill her, who did?"

Jude shrugged. "I don't know. I've had twenty years of sobriety to think about it. And now that I've heard Phoebe's description of the man she saw in her dream—well, there was one guy at the bar the night I was arrested who fits that description. Mean-looking fellow, an ex-con, I think." He paused. "There's no statute of limitations on murder, but we'd have to convince a judge of my innocence to reopen the case. I'm not sure a twenty-year-old memory from a girl who was five at the time would be compelling evidence."

"Still, we can try," Gram said.

Up till now, Gram had not spoken a single word—she had just sat there, stroking Jude's arm and trying not to cry. Now everyone turned to look at her. She was staring into his face, tears streaming steadily down her wrinkled cheeks.

"I'm so sorry," she whispered.

Jude clasped her hand. "Sorry for what, Mother?"

"Sorry I believed such a thing of you. Sorry I didn't trust my own son. I feel so . . . so *ashamed*."

Jude swallowed hard and put a hand under her chin, raising her eyes to meet his. "Given what I'd done in the past, you had every reason to believe I was guilty. I don't blame you, Mom." He smiled. "In fact, I need to thank you. For taking such good care of my little girl. For helping her grow up into a beautiful, intelligent, wonderful woman."

Jake shifted impatiently in his chair and cut a glance at Phoebe. "But you *confessed*. Sure, it wasn't exactly noble, getting drunk and running out on your daughter. Still, if you weren't guilty of murder, why did you say you were?"

"I was three sheets to the wind when they apprehended me. Apparently what I said was, 'It's all my fault.' And that was the truth."

"That's not a confession," Jake protested.

"To them it was. I had a record of abusing my wife. I ran. The murder weapon was the tire iron from my truck. I had used it a couple of days before, and must have left it in the grass outside the apartment. It had my fingerprints all over it."

"And so you went to prison for a crime you didn't commit," Jake said.

"When I came to my senses and realized I was going to be

convicted," Jude said, "it seemed—I don't know—fitting, some-how. A way to pay for everything I had done wrong."

Phoebe's eyes unfocused, she stared off into the distance, his final words echoing in her ears. Well, he *had* paid—with twenty years of his life. But he wasn't the only one. She had paid, too, with a wound that kept her separated from the people who loved her. Most of all, her mother had paid—the ultimate price, a violent and bloody end.

His twenty years wasn't nearly enough.

Phoebe grappled with the conflicting emotions that assaulted her. On the one hand, she wanted to reach out to him, broken and sad as he was, to tell him that she forgave him, and that she was glad to know he was innocent. But another part of her soul still burned with anger, a fury fueled by a lifetime of self-doubt. Even if he had not committed the heinous crime against her mother, Jude Lange was nevertheless responsible for everything Phoebe had endured for the past twenty years. He *wasn't* innocent. He was guilty. Guilty as sin.

She looked up to find Jake gazing intently at her. "Phoebe?"

She jumped up, jostling the table and sloshing coffee onto the place mat. "I . . . I need to be alone," she stammered. And she ran for the tower room as fast as her shaking legs would carry her.

⌒

"Phoebe!" Jake's muffled voice came through the heavy oak door. "Please, Phoebe, open up. Let me in."

"Go away."

"I'm not going away." He rapped his knuckles on the wood. "I want to talk to you."

"I don't want to talk to you," she said. "Or to anyone. Not right now."

A pause. "All right. I'll wait."

She heard a sliding noise, and then a soft thump on the floor of the hallway. He had to be kidding. He was going to sit there, outside her door, until she relented? Well, fine. He could wait until doomsday if he wanted.

Phoebe flung herself across the bed and put an arm over her eyes. She wished with all her being that she could just sleep, sink into oblivion—or even better, return to the dream-world where Jonathan and Lewis and Ethyle and Mildred waited for her. At least there, in the role of Great-Aunt Phoebe, she knew how to act, what to feel. At least there she had people around her who understood her and loved her.

No one in this reality could understand. Not Jake or Krista or Naomi. Not even Gram. How could any of them comprehend what she was feeling when she herself couldn't sort it out? Jonathan Barksdale's face rose up in her mind, and a wave of longing swept over her. If only she could talk to Jonathan, get his perspective on all of this.

She had wanted answers. Wanted things to be different. And although she had known, deep down, that she couldn't possibly change the past, she had at least hoped to make some improvement in the future.

Now things *had* changed, and with the revelation that her father had not, in fact, killed her mother, Phoebe found herself at a loss to know how to deal with that information. She had lived her whole life as an orphan. And now her father sat downstairs in this very house—not the murderer she had believed him to be, but a grief-stricken, heartbroken old man who had mistakenly thought he could pay for his misdeeds with twenty years of his life.

Phoebe stoutly resisted the urge to feel sorry for him. She didn't want pity or compassion clouding her mind and dissipating her anger. As long as she could blame him—

The conclusion to the thought came unbidden, Jonathan's gentle but persistent voice in the back of her mind: *As long as you can blame him, you don't have to take responsibility for yourself.*

She pushed the idea away. What responsibility? She wasn't responsible for her mother's death, or for her father's alcoholism. She had been the innocent victim.

But a victim of what? Jonathan's voice countered. *Of circumstance? Of a bent and broken world where terrible things happen?*

No. Phoebe couldn't—or wouldn't—accept that answer. She needed someone to blame, some flesh-and-blood person to hold accountable for the misery she had endured. Someone had to be responsible. Someone—

Let it go, Jonathan urged. *Open up. Forgive. Heal. You can do it. You did it once before.*

She closed her eyes and saw his face, gentle and entreating. But how could she possibly open up and heal now, after all these years? She had kept those wounds carefully covered, her soul pressed over them like a protective shroud. Alone, drawn in upon herself, she could keep her heart intact, so that no one, either human or divine, could touch her and hurt her again.

But you haven't been alone. Phoebe could almost see Jonathan smile. *You have a grandmother, a lover, faithful friends. And now, a father.*

She swallowed hard, and her eyes darted around the room. It was empty. No one was there with her, and yet she felt a presence—not just Jonathan's presence, but something more, something outside herself, but within. Shifting light through the tower window fell across the bed in bars.

Prison bars.

Suddenly Phoebe's mind flooded with images from her memory, both distant and recent: Gram, hugging her close in the middle of the night, rocking her, praying that prayer about ghoulies and ghosties and long-legged beasties. Jake's warm arms embracing her. Krista joking with her, laughing. Naomi leaning forward, nodding, listening intently. Jude Lange standing before her, holding out his hand, an expression of tremulous uncertainty on his stubbled face.

She stared at the bars of light across the comforter, and in that moment faced a truth she had never before been willing to confront. Her father was not the only one who had been incarcerated for the past twenty years. Phoebe, too, had been committed to a cell. A prison of her own making. A tomb.

And still the debt had not been paid. No amount of sacrifice could ever buy back what they had lost. Not her father's twenty years in jail, or her own two decades of confinement. Those years were gone, never to be called back again.

Jonathan's voice came again—quieter this time, almost a whisper. *Only the future can redeem the past. Unlock the cell. Roll back the stone. It's time to set the captives free.*

25

Interdependence Day

When Phoebe flipped the lock and pulled open the bedroom door, Jake fell backward onto the rug at her feet. He looked up at her and grinned sheepishly. "I said I'd wait."

"You've waited long enough." She held out a hand, helped him up, and led him into her room over to the rocking chair. "Sit," she commanded. "We need to talk."

Wordlessly he took his seat, and she perched on the edge of the bed across from him. She reached out, took his hands in hers, and stroked the veins that ran between his knuckles.

"When I was a little girl, I lived with the horror of watching my mother die. But I believed it was an accident. When the dreams began to come, and I saw someone else there in the room with her, I tried to push the truth away, to tell myself that it was a figment of my imagination. But I couldn't deny reality forever. It always comes back, and eventually it must be faced."

Jake nodded and squeezed her hand.

"All my life, I've wanted to alter the past," she went on quietly, not looking at him. "I wanted somehow, magically, to make this all go away. To change history, so I wouldn't be an orphan child. So I'd have a mother and a father. A family. A real family." She exhaled heavily. "But I couldn't change the past, and so instead I've kept myself—my heart, my soul—shut away from anything that could possibly wound me again."

"Like love?" he murmured.

Phoebe nodded. "When I came to after the concussion, the dream I'd had seemed so real, as if I'd really been there, back in 1927. In the dream, in the role of Great-Aunt Phoebe, I had taken the risk of being honest, of letting myself love and be loved. I felt free, liberated from the terrible burden of having to be strong and competent and independent. I didn't have to put on a facade in order for people to care for me and support me."

"And when you regained consciousness?" Jake prodded.

"I thought I could reproduce that liberation if I told you and Naomi and Krista what had been happening to me—the discovery that my father was Mama's murderer, and everything I had learned from Great-Aunt Phoebe's Memory Book and diary about that pattern of abuse. But—" She paused, groping for words.

"But it didn't work," Jake filled in for her.

Phoebe bit her lip. "No. I believed that if I told you what I knew, I would be set free from the bondage of the past. But there was more to it than just telling the story. Even as I tried to be honest, I was still holding back. I told the facts, but not the truth—the truth about myself."

Jake reached out and brushed an errant curl out of her eyes. "And what is the truth about yourself?"

"That I'm terrified. That I need other people, but I'm afraid that if they really know me they couldn't possibly love me. That I'm not strong and independent, the way I pretend to be. In many ways I'm still that frightened little five-year-old girl who doesn't want to be left alone."

"And that little girl is afraid of . . . ?"

Phoebe dragged her eyes away from his penetrating gaze. "Being weak. Being needy. Being—" A shudder ran through her as the full force of the awareness came. "Being abandoned."

Against her will, Phoebe began to cry. Jake slid out of the rocking chair and came to sit beside her on the bed. "This is so stupid," she muttered.

"No," he said. "There is nothing stupid about needing other people. We're made to be in relationship." He put his arms around her and drew her close. "I love you, Phoebe, and that means I need you. Not because I'm half a man without you, but because what you bring to my life enriches me, helps me become the person I was created to be. That's not weakness, Phoebe. It's strength. It's love. It's connectedness."

The tears came more forcefully, and Phoebe pulled away, just a little. "I've got to get a grip on myself."

"You've got to let it go," he corrected gently. "Don't hold it in. I suspect you haven't let yourself cry in a very long time."

His tenderness undid her, and Phoebe began to sob. She sagged against his shoulder and soaked his shirt. All the pain and anger that had been simmering inside her for years welled up and came out in a great wail. He held on while she cried and cried until she could cry no more.

At last her tears were spent, and she raised her head and gazed into his eyes. "Thank you," she murmured.

"For what?"

"For being here. For loving me. For . . . for everything. I love you so much, Jake. And I do need you."

He smiled and tightened his embrace. "That's good to hear. Because I intend to be around for a very, very long time."

26

Out of the Depths

Sunday morning dawned bright and sunny—a perfect, balmy June day in the mountains. It had been exactly one week since Phoebe had awakened in the hospital, and yet for all that had transpired since then, it might have been a year.

Phoebe's journal lay on the bedside table. She picked it up and thumbed through her entries for the week. She had written more in the past few days than she thought humanly possible. All that anger, rage, loneliness, and insecurity scrawled over the pages. All her feelings about her life, her isolation, her father, her unwillingness to open herself to others. It was a messy, disturbing business, this facing of the truth. But she had at last come to a place of resolution, and of peace.

All the ends weren't neatly tied up, of course. Life wasn't like that. She would never have answers to some of her questions. But she had begun the process of forgiving her father, of releasing both him and herself from the emotional prison she had created over the years. She was trying to learn to trust. To believe in second chances.

Jake had contacted a lawyer friend of his, a bright young criminal attorney from Raleigh who had listened intently to the story and agreed to represent Phoebe's father in clearing his name and re-opening the investigation. Twenty years was a long time, and there were no guarantees, he'd said. Still, they would try. The real killer might never be brought to justice, but for the time being, Phoebe was content with knowing who *didn't* commit the heinous crime.

Looking down into the garden behind the tower bedroom, Phoebe could see the azaleas budding and purple-bearded irises poking out of the mulch to rise in glory against the wall of the garage. Perhaps later today she would bring a chair outside so Gram could enjoy the day while Phoebe spent some time clearing away weeds and setting the garden to rights. A fitting gesture, Phoebe thought, a visible symbol of what had been going on inside of her.

A light knock on the door drew her attention from the window. "Yes?"

The door opened. "May I come in for a moment?"

Phoebe turned. In the doorway stood her father, dressed in a gray suit, white shirt, and burgundy bow tie. His hair had been trimmed, and the stubbly beard was gone. His complexion had lost some of its sallowness, and his brown eyes glowed warmly.

"Jude!" She faltered, not knowing what to call him. "You look—well, downright handsome."

He tugged at his lapels and tactfully ignored her discomfort. "I clean up pretty good."

"You certainly do. What's the occasion?"

"Occasion?" He tilted his head. "It's Sunday. The general opinion seems to be that we'd all go to church, and then go out for dinner afterward."

"Well, I . . . ah, all right," Phoebe stammered. "It's just that I didn't think you'd—"

"Didn't think I'd turn out to be a churchgoing kind of man?" He smiled and perched on the edge of the rocking chair like a small bird clinging to a swinging bough. "I learned a few things in prison—things I might not have learned anywhere else."

Intrigued, Phoebe settled on the bed and waited expectantly.

"In prison, a man can go one of two ways," he mused. "He can bang his head against the bars and become his worst self, letting anger and pain and self-righteousness rule his soul. Or he can let the cage set him free."

Phoebe smiled. "'Stone walls do not a prison make, Nor iron bars a cage,'" she quoted.

"What's that?"

"A poem. Richard Lovelace. Seventeenth century."

"Ah, yes." He pinched the bridge of his nose with two fingers. "My educated daughter. Sounds like a poem I might could understand—you'll have to read it to me sometime."

"I will. But go on. You were talking about the cage setting you free."

"Right. When I was convicted, it seemed fitting—a way to pay for what I'd done. It didn't matter that I hadn't committed the crime that put me away. I had a lot of other things to atone for. But gradually I began to realize that nothing I ever sacrificed would be enough. And I began to see better reasons for being behind bars."

Phoebe leaned forward. "Such as?"

"Do you remember the old song, 'Me and Bobby McGee'?" When she shook her head, he sighed. "Ah, you're too young. It's a folk song from the sixties. There's this one line in it that has always stuck in my mind—'Freedom's just another word for nothin' left to lose.' Well, in prison, you've got nothing left to lose, either. It makes you start thinking about what's really important in life."

"And what is important?"

"Love. Family. God."

Phoebe snapped to attention. "God?"

He chuckled. "Yes, God. God is in prison, too—maybe more often than in some churches. The chaplain gave me a Bible, and I started reading it out of sheer boredom. That's the real punishment, you know—all those hours of being locked up with nothing to do. I didn't understand a lot of what I read, but I did get one thing. I found out why my sacrifice of twenty years was not enough to put my soul back on track.

"They had an AA meeting in the prison," he went on. "Alcoholics Anonymous." He shook his head and laughed.

"Although it wasn't very anonymous, since we all knew each other. Anyway, when they started talking about connecting with your Higher Power, the pieces fell in place for me—and not just about dealing with my alcoholism. About everything. There wasn't enough will power in the world to fix what was wrong with me. I needed something more. Someone else."

"And that someone was God."

"Yes. At first I didn't think I was worthy of God's love and forgiveness. And I was right. But the love and forgiveness came anyway. It didn't take away my responsibility for what I did in this life—AA forces you to face yourself. Still, accepting God's forgiveness set me free, made me a different man than I had been when I went in."

He dug in his pocket and came up with a small round coin. "My twenty-year token," he said, holding it up to the light. "I keep it in my pocket, where I can feel it and remind myself how much grace is available to anybody who's willing to receive it."

The warm brown eyes lingered on Phoebe's face. "I appreciate what you're doing, how you're trying, Phoebe. But I also want you to know that I don't expect anything from you," he said. "You've been without a father all your life. I know I can't simply reappear in your life and pick up as if nothing ever happened. I just want to ask one small favor."

"What favor?"

"Give me a chance to prove myself to you—not as a father, necessarily, but as a friend."

Phoebe averted her face to hide the tears that had sprung to her eyes, then thought better of it and turned to look at him again. "Agreed," she said. "Now, out." She pointed toward the door.

"You're throwing me out?"

She grinned. "I am. Go on, or I'll never be ready for church in time."

~

It had been years since Phoebe had set foot in the small brick church on Merrimon Avenue, but it could have been yesterday. The same contingent of white-haired ladies still filled Widow's Row, the fourth pew from the back on the left side. People still milled about, greeting one another with hugs and kisses and handshakes, right up until the organist played the opening bars of the prelude.

Gram pointed to an empty pew on the right, and Phoebe slid in next to Jake. She settled herself, glanced over the bulletin, then looked down the row. What a contingent they made, the seven of them! Even Hargraves had come and sat on the far end next to Phoebe's father, engaging him in an animated conversation. Next to him, Krista craned her neck to look around and Naomi poked her in the ribs to get her to sit still. Jake sat close beside Phoebe, and on the other side, Gram patted her knee and smiled at her.

"Thank you for coming," Gram whispered in her ear. "I'm so glad you're here."

"I'm glad, too," Phoebe said, not quite sure she meant it, but wanting it to be true. Then she caught a glimpse of her grandmother's left cheek. "Gram, turn your head. You've got something on your face."

"I get a lot of hugs and kisses when I come to church," Gram said happily.

"Yes, you do. That's because everybody loves you so much." She fished in her purse for a tissue and wiped off the bright pink lipstick smear. The action evoked a wave of tenderness in Phoebe, and she laid her palm briefly against the soft, wrinkled face. She couldn't imagine, now, how she had ever felt alone and abandoned with someone like Gram in her life.

She looked to her right, where Jake and Krista and Naomi sat. And beyond them, her father, brought back as from the dead. How rich she was, and how blessed with people who cared for her. Love such as theirs should have made her complete. They were family. She belonged. Why, then, did she still feel not quite whole?

The opening hymn began, and in a flash of insight Phoebe received her answer. *Great is thy faithfulness, O God my Father . . .*

That was it. The missing piece. She longed for an experience of God's faithfulness. It wasn't enough to believe in God with the simple trust of childhood, or to dip into theological debate, or to throw out a challenge prayer from a vantage point of anger and pain. She needed more—a sense of the Presence, a real, palpable nearness, an assurance. The kind of assurance she had felt vicariously through Great-Aunt Phoebe's diary and the dream.

But where was it to come from? And how would she know it if she found it?

The pastor stepped into the pulpit, preparing to deliver a sermon entitled "Here in This Community." Phoebe forced herself to focus.

He was a youngish man, not more than forty, tall and lean with thinning blond hair, thick glasses, and a bushy mustache. Not handsome by conventional standards, or particularly dynamic. He was, in fact, rather soft-spoken and unassuming, even shy. But there was something about him—an earnestness, an authenticity—that Phoebe found compelling.

And he was speaking directly to her.

"We look at the Scriptures," he said, "and see example after example of the miraculous work of God in people's lives. Moses heard God in the burning bush, and again on the mountain. Angels came to Abraham to give him direction. Mary and Joseph and the shepherds who attended Jesus' birth all had miraculous manifestations of the Divine to cling to. Even the Magi had a star.

"In the days of Jesus' ministry on earth, the disciples walked with their Messiah. They had a flesh-and-blood incarnation to touch and hear and see. We read those stories and wonder where in the twenty-first century—in this age of incredulity and skepticism—can we find such certainty, such assurance, such tangible evidence of Immanuel, God with us?

"The Epistle lesson for today gives us a hint: *We* are the body of Christ. *We* are the continuing incarnation of the Divine. Look around and see Jesus. We who believe and trust and love each other are the manifestation of God in this place, at this time . . ."

Phoebe heard little of the rest of the sermon. Her mind went into a tailspin, and deep in her soul, she felt a stirring resonance with this truth, a bell tolling the advent of a new day.

The sermon was over, and around her people began stirring, flipping pages, rising to their feet as the organist played the opening chords of the final hymn. She edged close to Jake and looked at the page in the hymnbook. It was a song she had never heard before, and so she listened as the words swirled around her and through her on the rising and falling cadences of the tune:

> *Out of the depths, O God, we call to you.*
> *Wounds of the past remain, affecting all we do.*
> *Facing our lives, we need your love so much.*
> *Here in this community, heal us by your touch.*

Phoebe had barely read past the first line when her eyes clogged with tears and the print blurred in front of her. She had not prayed, had not technically asked for a response from God, and yet here it was, right in front of her.

> *Out of the depths of fear, O God, we speak.*
> *Breaking the silences, the searing truth we seek.*

Safe among friends, our grief and rage we share.
Here in this community, hold us in your care.

By now she was crying openly, tears streaking down her face and dripping onto Jake's sleeve. She didn't try to stop them. Not this time.

God of the loving heart, we praise your name.
Dance through our lives and loves; anoint with
   Spirit's flame.
Your light illumines each familiar face.
Here in this community, meet us with your grace.

Jake shifted the hymnal to the other side, grasped her hand, and held on as deep inside Phoebe's soul—in that dark and hollow place she had kept sealed for so many years—something broke loose.

No earthquake, no tongues of fire. No mighty rushing wind or angels singing. Only a breath of fresh air as the door of the tomb rolled open.

Epilogue

Phoebe stood at the window of the tower bedroom, looking down into the garden below. She could see the top of her grandmother's wide-brimmed straw hat, with wisps of gray hair escaping around the neck of her faded denim work shirt. A profusion of purple irises rose against the sun-splashed wall, and tulips and lilies grew in clumps among the boulders of the rock garden and in borders around the dogwood trees.

Phoebe raised the window and leaned her elbows on the sill. "Don't overdo, Gram."

The old woman rocked back on her haunches, swiped her brow with a gloved hand, and shaded her eyes to look upward. "Quit fussing over me, Phoebe. I'm fine. Wonderful, in fact. Have you ever seen such a glorious day?"

Phoebe lifted her face to the cloudless sky, a deep, clear Carolina blue. Blue like a robin's egg. Blue like the snow on a moonlit night. Blue like the light in her true love's eyes. Sunshine ricocheted off the diamond that adorned her left hand and scattered glints of splintered light everywhere. She lowered her gaze again. "The garden's beautiful."

Gram jerked up a handful of weeds and tossed them into the wheelbarrow. "It had better be beautiful—my one and only granddaughter is getting married here one week from today."

Phoebe felt a rush of pleasure surge through her veins, and she smiled. "Do you want some help?"

Gram shook her head. "Jake's gone to the co-op to get some mulch. He's quite the able assistant. We'll be done shortly."

"All right. I'll leave you to it, then."

Phoebe shut the window and went back to the desk—Great-Aunt Phoebe's desk, the one she had found in a corner of the attic and brought down to its rightful place in the tower bedroom. Spread across the top was her great-aunt's diary, the Memory Book, and a shoe box full of old photographs.

She had sorted through until she found what she wanted. The picture of Great-Aunt Phoebe and Little Lewis on the front porch of the house. A similar one, some thirty years later, of Lewis as an adult, standing in virtually the same position with a small boy at his side. Jude. Her father. And a third—a smiling, brown-haired woman with her arms wrapped around a little girl. Phoebe's mother, Marie, and Phoebe herself at age four.

She picked up this last photograph and stared at it. Mama had looked so fresh and young, so innocent. So . . . happy.

Phoebe's eyes drifted to the other pictures, all taken on the same porch from almost the same vantage point. Her mind stacked them up like transparencies, each face overlapping the others. Great-Aunt Phoebe, and Grandpa, and Mama. Little Lewis, and Little Jude, and Little Phoebe.

At last, all the pieces of the puzzle fit. Some of the shards of her history were sharp and jagged, able to cut the heart and draw blood. Some were gentle and rounded, easy to handle. But all fit together to create the larger picture. A family, drawn together by a common heritage, common struggles, a common life.

She fished a glue stick out of the top drawer and fixed the photographs into the last blank pages of the Memory Book. Below each, she wrote the appropriate captions:

Phoebe Lange (Great-Aunt Phoebe),
age 18, with little brother Lewis, age 6.

Lewis Lange, age 35, with son Jude, age 8.

Marie Lange (Jude's wife), age 31,
with daughter Phoebe, age 4.

Phoebe paused. Three pictures on two pages. And a blank space, as if waiting to be filled by another photograph, another generation. They had come full circle, but this was not an end. It was only a beginning.

She thought for a minute, took up the pen, and wrote across the bottom of the page:

This is my great-aunt Phoebe's Memory Book. From it, and from her, I learned that the past is the key to the future. We cannot escape who we are, but we can change. With God's help and each other's support, we can inaugurate new patterns—patterns of love and trust and commitment, patterns of healing and forgiveness. To that end, I offer this prayer:

God of the loving heart, we praise your name.
Dance through our lives and loves; anoint with Spirit's flame.
Your light illumines each familiar face.
Here in this community, meet us with your grace.

Phoebe Lange, June 2001

~

The dream came again, but this time Phoebe knew it was a dream.

Little Lewis came to stand at the side of her bed, his wide dark eyes gazing at her, his Buster Brown haircut ruffling slightly, as if a breeze were coming through the open window. He was just as she remembered him, in a white collarless shirt and knickers held up with suspenders.

And he was smiling.

Behind him, Jonathan stood near the doorway, twirling a gray fedora in both hands. A little to one side, as if in bas-relief, she could see Ethyle and Mildred, their arms linked together. They were both gazing at her. Mildred held a handkerchief to her temple as if she'd been crying.

"Go on," Jonathan urged Lewis.

The boy leaned in close and twined his arms around Phoebe's neck. "I love you, Phoebe," he whispered. "And I need to tell you something."

"I love you, too, sweetie," she responded. "What did you want to tell me?"

"That I'm going to be all right. We're all going to be all right. You'll see."

Phoebe sat up and gathered him into her arms, stroking his hair and planting kisses on the top of his head. "I know," she said. "I'm not afraid anymore."

He hugged her fiercely, then disentangled himself from her embrace and stepped back. "Don't forget me, Sis," he said, his voice tight.

"Are you going somewhere?"

"No." He looked down at his shoes. "You are."

Phoebe's heart lurched. "Where am I going?"

"Away. But you'll be fine. You have lots of people who love you." He raised his head, and she could see tears standing in his eyes. Behind him, Ethyle and Mildred were waving, growing dimmer, as if their images were being diluted. Lewis backed up toward the door and reached for Jonathan's hand. "Good-bye."

"Don't go!" Phoebe called.

Lewis grinned and swiped at his cheek with a fist. "Remember me, Phoebe."

"I'll always remember you, Lewis," she said. "And you, Jonathan."

Jonathan gave a jaunty salute and nodded. Something was happening, something she couldn't quite understand. Ethyle and Mildred had almost disappeared. Jonathan and Lewis were becoming fainter, more transparent. She could still see them, but she could also see through them, as through a foggy glass. Like images of ice against the wallpaper and the doorpost.

"Thank you," she whispered. "Thank you for changing everything. I'll never be the same."

"You've changed us, too," Jonathan said, his voice hollow and distant. "I'll love you forever. We'll be with you. Always. In your heart."

Then they were gone, vanished like a mist, like an echo on the wind.

But the love remained.